Caroline Anderson is a matriarch, writer, armchair gardener, unofficial tearoom researcher and eater of lovely cakes. Not necessarily in that order! *What Caroline loves:* her family. Her friends. Reading. Writing contemporary love stories. Hearing from readers. Walks by the sea with coffee/ice cream/cake thrown in! Torrential rain. Sunshine in spring/autumn. *What Caroline hates:* losing her pets. Fighting with her family. Cold weather. Hot weather. Computers. Clothes shopping. *Caroline's plans:* keep smiling and writing!

THE MIDWIFE'S LONGED-FOR BABY

BY
CAROLINE ANDERSON

MILLS & BOON

First published in Great Britain 2017
by Mills & Boon, an imprint of HarperCollins*Publishers*
1 London Bridge Street, London, SE1 9GF

Large Print edition 2018

© 2017 Caroline Anderson

ISBN: 978-0-263-07261-7

MIX
Paper from
responsible sources
FSC™ C007454

This book is produced from independently certified FSC™ paper to ensure responsible forest management. For more information visit www.harpercollins.co.uk/green.

Printed and bound in Great Britain
by CPI Group (UK) Ltd, Croydon, CR0 4YY

34755071

For all those whose infertility stories
have touched my heart, and for the
very many more whose stories I have
never heard but who are themselves
travelling this emotionally challenging road
with courage. My heart aches for you.

CHAPTER ONE

'LIV, HAVE YOU got a minute?'

She hesitated, about to say no, but Ben wasn't one to waste time and if he wanted to talk to her...

'If it really is only that? I need to check on a mum soon.'

'That's fine, it won't take long. I just want to run something by you. Can we go in my office?'

His office?

'Is this about Jen?' she asked as Ben closed the door.

The fleeting smile didn't quite reach his eyes. 'In a way. Did you know she's got cancer?'

'Yes, Simon told me yesterday. I was gutted. She's such a lovely person and it seems so unfair. He said they're moving home so their families can help with the children while she's having treatment. So what is it you want me to do?' she asked, thinking flowers, a gift voucher, something for the kids—

'Nothing, but what I do could affect you, because yesterday was Simon's last day and his compassionate leave's pretty open-ended so we need a locum, and I'd like to talk to Nick about it.'

'Nick?'

Of all the things he'd been going to say, her ex husband's name was so far down the list it wasn't even on it, and just the sound of his name made her heart beat faster. And he wasn't officially ex, because she'd never quite been able to follow through on that—

'Are you still in touch?'

Ben nodded. 'Yes, we're in touch. I speak to him quite often. He always asks about you,' he added gently.

Her heart lurched. 'Does he? How is he?' she asked, trying not to sound too needy and failing hopelessly.

'He's OK. He's well, keeps himself busy.' He frowned, hesitating, then went on, 'I know it's none of my business, Liv, and I'm not asking any questions, but I was really sorry when you two split up.'

She felt her eyes fill and blinked as she looked away. 'Me, too, but it wasn't working.' Any more than this was, this awful aching emptiness where her love for Nick had been...

'I know. I could see there was something wrong, so I wasn't surprised, just saddened for you both. Look, don't worry about it. I'll try and get someone else. I only thought of him because he'd be perfect for the job, but I don't want to make things difficult for you—for either of you, really.'

The shock had worn off now, swamped by a tidal wave of mixed emotions that she couldn't quite work out. Longing? Dread? She didn't have a clue. Both, maybe, but confusion was fighting its way to the top of the pile.

'I don't understand how he could do it anyway. Doesn't he have a job?'

He must have. He was paying the mortgage on their house—

'Not any more, as far as I know. His existing locum post's about to come to an end and I haven't heard that he's got anything else lined up so I wanted to get in soon if we were to stand a chance, but it's probably too late anyway.'

He was *locuming*? He'd been made a consultant at Yoxburgh Park Hospital a few months before they'd split up. How had he ended up working as a locum? Although it was only a year ago since he'd left. Maybe nothing had come up, nothing as good anyway. Nothing that would do him justice…

'Can I think about it? Before you ask him, or get anyone else. It's just—it's the last thing I expected you to say and I can't quite get my head round it.'

'I know, I can see that. And I realise you might need to talk to him first.'

No way. She hadn't spoken to him since that horrible day that she'd regretted ever since, but this wasn't the time or the way to do it. She shook her head. 'No, I don't need to do that. How long can I have?'

Ben shrugged. 'The rest of the morning? I'm sorry, I know it isn't long, but if you think you can deal with it I really don't want to hang about in case we lose him. It's right up his street— mostly obstetrics, but there's some of the fertility clinic work as well, which is why I thought of him.'

That stopped her mind in its tracks, and she felt her jaw drop. She just couldn't picture him in a fertility clinic, of all the ironic places, but of course Simon's job partly involved it.

'I didn't realise he knew anything at all about infertility.'

Apart from their own, but she wasn't saying that to Ben.

'Yes, that's one of the reasons why we want him, because of Simon's role here. Plus he's a damn good obstetrician, of course, but he's a perfect fit. He's been running the fertility clinic in his hospital since last May, and it shuts any day now.'

Her heart was beating so fast she could feel it thudding against her ribs. Of all the things for him to do, running a fertility clinic was so out of left field she'd never have seen it coming. Why would he choose to punish himself in that way? *Unless he'd had no choice.* Had he been driven to it just to earn a living? Her guilt over the mortgage ramped up a notch.

'I had no idea,' she said numbly. She took another moment, letting it all sink in a little, and then took a deep breath and made a decision she just hoped she didn't regret.

'Talk to him, Ben. Ask him if he's interested. If he is—well, I'm sure we can be civilised about it.'

'Are you sure? I realise it's a big decision for you.'

'But it isn't really mine to make. It's yours, and his, and if he's the right man for the job, who am I to stand in the way? And anyway, it's not permanent. Ask him, Ben. Just keep me in the loop, OK? I don't want any surprises.'

'Of course I will.' He opened the door and stared down thoughtfully into her eyes. 'Thank you, Liv. I do appreciate it and I know it can't be easy for you.'

Did he? She wondered how much he knew about their break-up, about the why and the how. Had Nick spoken to him about it? Surely not. If there was one thing her marriage had taught her, it was that Nick didn't talk about his feelings. Not to her, and certainly not to his boss.

She found a smile from somewhere. 'You're welcome. Just let me know his reaction.'

'I will.'

* * *

'Nick? It's Ben Walker. Are you OK to talk? I want to ask you something.'

'Yeah, sure. What d'you want to know?' he asked.

'Nothing. I'm headhunting you. I know your clinic's shutting any time now, and we need a full-time locum consultant to cover Obs and Gynae and some of the fertility clinic workload and I thought it sounded right up your street, unless you've got your next job lined up already?'

Ben was asking him to go back? With Liv still there? At least, he assumed she was. He hadn't heard otherwise and Ben would have told him, he was sure. Would he be working with her?

His heart rate rocketed, and he hauled in a deep breath and let it go, consciously engaging his brain instead of his adrenal glands.

'Whose job is it? It sounds like Simon's.'

'It is. His wife's got cancer and he's gone off on compassionate leave with immediate effect. They're moving back to their home town so their parents can help with childcare.'

'Oh, no, that's horrendous. Poor Jen. Poor all of them. And poor you, because it's obviously left you in the lurch, but I'm not sure I'm the man for the job. Does Liv know you're asking me?'

'Yes. I asked her first. She said she thought you could be civilised about it.'

Civilised?

He'd be right under her nose, working with couples to solve the very thing that had left their marriage in tatters. *Civilised* wasn't the word he would have applied to that situation.

A minefield, more likely.

Or an opportunity to build bridges? He knew so much more now than he had then, but the pain was still raw and no amount of knowledge was going to make that go away.

Could he do it? It wasn't as if they'd be working together, and it was only temporary in any case. They could keep out of each other's way if necessary, but it might give them a chance—

'So, are you still free?'

'Yes, technically. I haven't got anything lined up yet, at least, and I'm seeing the last patients today, but I had thought I'd take a break. When would you want me to start?'

Ben made a sound that could have been laughter. 'Tomorrow? And by the way, that was a joke, but—ASAP, really. We can cover it for a few days but after that it'll get really tricky. Every woman in Suffolk seems to be pregnant or trying to be at the moment.'

His chest tightened. Not quite every woman. Not his Liv...

'Why don't you come and talk to me about it?' Ben went on. 'See how you feel?'

He had no idea how he'd feel. Confused? Desperate to see Liv? Afraid to see her, to find that she was happily settled without him when he was still miserable and lonely and struggling to make sense of it all? But maybe she *was* happy, which would mean he'd done the right thing by leaving without a fight. Maybe he needed to know that so he could move on?

There was no real reason why he couldn't go. When the clinic closed its doors at five that evening, he'd be jobless. He'd planned a holiday, something reckless and adrenaline-soaked, but he hadn't booked anything and now Ben was dangling this opportunity to go back to Yoxburgh right in front of his nose.

Yoxburgh, and Liv.

They'd been so happy there at first in the pretty Victorian seaside town, but it had all gone horribly wrong for them and now the only memories he had of it were sad ones. Did he really want to go back?

He'd made changes in his life, tried to get it back on track, but although his diet and lifestyle had undergone a radical overhaul, his heart hadn't moved on. He'd just shut it away, buried it under a massive pile of work and endless runs around an inner-city park, and going back was bound to open a whole new can of worms. Did he really want to do that? The sensible answer was no—or was that just the coward's answer?

And Ben needed him. He had no commitments or ties, no reason why he couldn't go, except that Liv would be there, and maybe that wasn't a good enough reason to stay away.

Even though it was a minefield, even though they hadn't spoken in over a year, even though he knew it was rash and stupid and ill-considered, he realised there was a massive part of him that wanted to see her again.

Needed to see her again.

It was high time they had the conversation he'd

been putting off since they'd split up. The conversation he owed her—and the one she owed him, like why after more than a year she still hadn't started divorce proceedings...

'Let's just go for it,' he said, suddenly decisive. 'I can't do tomorrow, but why don't I come up on Friday? That gives me a day to tidy up here and pack, and if I can sort everything out with your HR first thing on Friday morning I can start work right away. My paperwork's all in order, so once HR have seen it I'll be good to go. Then you'll only have to deal with tomorrow, and I can spend the weekend finding somewhere to live.'

'Are you sure?'

'Yes, absolutely,' he said without giving himself time to back out of it. 'Let's do it. I'll drive down early so I'm with you for eight and I can be in HR as soon as they open.'

'Nick, thank you. I can't tell you how grateful I am,' Ben said, and the relief in his voice made Nick realise just how much pressure his old clinical lead was under. 'And don't worry about finding anywhere to live,' Ben added, 'you can stay with us as long as you need to, Daisy'd love to have you. Come here, to the hospital. You know where to find me. They'll page me when you get here.'

'Sure. Thanks. I'll see you then.'

He hung up, slid the phone into his pocket and stared blankly across the room.

He was going back.

He wasn't sure he was ready to see Liv again, because he'd never managed to get any emotional distance and his heart was still as raw as it had been the day she threw him out, so it was going to be tough. Very tough. But maybe he could use the opportunity to find out if she was happy without him, because he sure as hell wasn't happy without her...

There was a knock on the door and a nurse popped her head into the room. 'Mr Jarvis? Mr and Mrs Lyons are waiting to see you.'

He nodded, gave himself a mental shake and got to his feet. 'Show them in, please.'

He was coming back today.

Taking Simon's job, at least in the short term. She still couldn't work out how she felt about that. Confused, more than anything. Confused and nervous and tingling with apprehension. Lots of that.

She found a slot in the staff car park, got out and headed for the maternity unit on autopilot, her mind whirling.

Would she see him today? Did she want to? Did *he* want to see *her*? Their last exchange had hardly been amicable. Well, her side of it anyway. He'd hardly said a word but then he hadn't needed to, the evidence had spoken for itself.

She reached the kerb and glanced up, checking that the road was clear, and saw a car approaching.

Nick's car.

She recognised it instantly, and her heart started to thud as he drew closer, their eyes meeting as he slowed down.

To speak to her?

For a moment she thought he was going to stop, and then he raised his hand in acknowledgement and drove on, and she hauled in a breath and crossed the road on legs like jelly.

Her heart was tumbling in her chest, her lips dry, and she was breathing so fast she could have been running. Ridiculous. He was just a doctor, here to do his job, and she was just a midwife doing hers. The fact that they were still married was neither here nor there. They could do this.

She just had to work out how.

Nick parked the car and sat there for a moment, waiting for his heart to slow down.

He'd known it would be odd to see her again, but he hadn't expected the thunderbolt that had struck him when he'd met her eyes. It was like being punched in the gut, and it had taken his breath away.

Jaws clenched, he took the key out of the ignition, picked up the briefcase containing his stethoscope and the file with all the documentation for HR and got out of the car, following her towards the maternity unit.

Why the hell had he said yes? He could have turned Ben down, walked away, gone and had the holiday he'd been promising himself. Then he wouldn't have been here, he wouldn't have seen her and ripped open the wound left by the abrupt end to their marriage.

Not that it had taken much ripping. It had barely skinned over in the last year and a bit, but he was here now, the damage was done and he might as well just get on with it. And anyway, she needed the truth. They both did, and maybe then they could both move on.

The door slid open and he strode through it, went up to the maternity reception desk and asked them to page Ben.

'Morning, all.'

'Oh, Liv, I'm so glad I've caught you. Can you do us a huge favour? Would you mind covering an antenatal clinic this morning? Jan's called in sick and you're the only person who's not already involved in a delivery.'

She felt a little shaft of relief and smiled at her line manager. 'No, that's fine, I'll head straight down.' And she'd be nicely tucked out of the way so she wouldn't run the risk of bumping into Nick.

Which was stupid, really, because it was going to happen sometime, but she'd had less than forty-eight hours to get used to the idea of him coming back and judging by her reaction to him in the car park, it had been nothing like long enough.

She'd spend the morning giving herself a thorough talking-to, and then by the time he actually started work she'd have herself firmly under control.

Good plan.

Except it wasn't.

The clinic receptionist welcomed her with a smile of relief and then comprehensively trashed her peace of mind.

'Thank heavens it's you, Liv, we need someone who knows the ropes. There's a bit of a delay because the locum who's covering for Mr Bailey is still in HR, but he'll be down soon, apparently, so if you could make a start that would be amazing.'

Simon's clinic? That meant she'd be working with Nick all morning, before she had a chance to shore up the walls and get all her defences in place. Great. Fabulous.

Her heart had started to pound, and she hauled in a breath, picked up the first set of notes with shaking hands and pasted on a smile.

'No problem. I can do that,' she said, as much to herself as the receptionist. She walked out to the waiting area, glanced at the file and scanned the room.

'Judy Richards?'

'Nick! Welcome back!'

He recognised Jane, the motherly but ruthlessly efficient woman who acted as Ben's secretary as well as Simon's, and greeted her warmly.

'Hello, Jane, it's good to see you again. How are you?'

'I'm fine. I've been expecting you. HR said you'd be up here shortly. They said you were very well organised, ironically.'

He laughed. 'It just so happens I had a file ready with the relevant paperwork in it because I knew I'd need it soon, but don't let that lull you into a false sense of security. I hate admin.'

She smiled knowingly. 'I haven't forgotten that. Don't worry, I'll make sure you do everything you have to do.'

'Can you read my mind?' he asked, and she just laughed.

'If necessary. That's what I'm here for.'

'Good. I don't suppose you've got Simon's schedule handy, have you? I really need to hit the ground running. Ben said something about a clinic and I've got a list this afternoon.'

'Yes, I've printed it all out for you here. First on your list is the antenatal clinic, as you know. It's still in the same place and they're expecting you. And your elective list starts at two, so you should just about have time after the clinic to meet your patients before you start in Theatre. The notes are on the ward.'

'Jane, you're a legend.' He hung his stethoscope round his neck, left his briefcase in her care and went.

At least in the clinic he was less likely to run into Liv, because she'd be safely tucked away on the midwife-led unit. And even though in a way he'd wanted to see her, their brief encounter this morning had shaken him more than he'd expected and he could do without any more surprises.

Yes, a nice, busy clinic was exactly what he needed. Just until he got his head round the idea of working in the same building as her...

'Liv...'

She was standing in the empty corridor with

an armful of notes when she heard him say her name, and she turned slowly and met his eyes.

Anguish, love, regret—and then nothing, as he got control of himself again and slammed the shutters down. He'd had plenty of practice at that, he'd got it down to a fine art in the last year of their marriage, but he'd been too slow this time and his reaction exactly mirrored her own.

'Hello, Nick,' she said, her voice sounding scratchy and unused. The words *how are you* hovered on her tongue, but she couldn't speak because it had glued itself to the roof of her mouth so she just stared at him.

His face was leaner, she realised, the crows' feet more pronounced, the frown lines shallower. Because he was happier? He hadn't looked happy, but he looked more like the old Nick, the man she'd fallen in love with, fit and well and healthy but with a touch of grey at his temples now. Stress, or just age? He was thirty-nine now, nearly forty, and he wore it well apart from that.

Not that the silver threaded through his dark hair did anything to dim his subtle but potent sex appeal—

Her heart was beating so fast it was deafening

her, her breath was lodged in her throat, and she had to clamp her lips together to stifle a sudden little sob.

She blinked fiercely and adjusted the folders in her arms before looking back at him, and as she met those beautiful, smoky grey eyes again her heart thudded, but his gaze held her eyes and she was powerless to look away.

'I wasn't expecting to see you down here,' he said after a second of silence that seemed to scream on for eternity, and his gruff voice set her free and she breathed again.

'Ditto, but it's just as well you're here now, we've got a lot of work to do.' She pretended to look at the notes in her arms. Anything to get away from those searching eyes when her own were bound to be too revealing. 'I take it you managed to tick all HR's boxes?'

'Yes. I have a file I keep up to date. It comes in handy when you're a locum.'

That again. *Why hasn't he got a full-time job?*

He hesitated, as if there was something else he wanted to say, but after a moment he looked down at the armful of folders she was holding. 'So, what's that lot?'

'The ladies who've had their BP and fundal height measured and their urine tested, so they're all ready for you.' Her voice was almost normal again, and she nearly laughed. If he had any idea what was going on in her chest—

She led him into the consulting room and handed him the folders, and as he took them his hand brushed lightly against hers and the heat from his skin sent a wave of longing through her. She almost dropped the files but he had them, and he turned swiftly away and dumped them on the desk.

'Anyone I should be particularly aware of?' he asked, his voice a little taut and very business-like, so she followed his lead. Anything to help get herself back under control before her heart gave out.

'Yes, Judy Richards,' she said briskly. 'She has a history of early miscarriage. This is her fourth pregnancy, she's thirty-two weeks which is the longest she's ever gone, but her fundal height hasn't changed since her last appointment a week ago and that wasn't as much as it should have been, so it might be that the baby's found a new position, or it could be that it's stopped growing for some reason. She's on the top of the pile.'

He frowned thoughtfully, all business now. 'Right. Good. Has she been tested for APS?'

'Yes, after her last miscarriage. The test came back negative.'

'Hmm. OK, well, she'd better have another scan before I see her, if we can do it without worrying her too much.'

'It's done. I knew you'd ask for it so I told her it was because it was a new consultant, and she didn't question it. The results are on here,' she said, handing him the department tablet.

'Great. Thanks.' He scrolled through and studied the results, then handed it back, frowning thoughtfully.

'OK. I think I'm going to admit her. Can you call her in, please, and I'll check her over and break the news?'

'Sure.'

And oddly it was fine, because Judy Richards and her baby needed them, they had a job to do and so they just got on with it, slipping seamlessly back into the familiar routine as if it had been yesterday. Not that she was relaxed in any way, but it was a joy watching him with Judy, and a stark reminder of how good he was at his job.

She'd forgotten how intuitive a doctor he was, and how caring. Kind, gentle, thorough—and from his first greeting onwards, Liv could see Judy had utter faith in him.

'Mrs Richards—I'm Nick Jarvis, I've taken over from Simon Bailey. I've had a look at your notes, and also the scan you had done today. It doesn't really shed any light—which is good news in a way, I suppose, but it still leaves some unanswered questions and I don't like that, so I think I'd like to admit you and do a few more tests, get a closer look at your baby and the placenta and retest you for APS—antiphospholipid syndrome. Has anybody discussed that with you yet?'

'Yes, Mr Bailey did, but he didn't think I'd got it.'

'He may well be right, but I'm erring on the side of caution, so if that's all right with you, I'll ring the ward and make the arrangements for you to be admitted now, and then maybe someone could bring some things in for you later.'

'I can't go home and get them myself?'

'You can, of course, but I'd like to get the tests under way as soon as possible and I'm in Theatre this afternoon, so I'd very much rather you didn't because I'd like to look after you myself rather than hand you over to someone else in my team.'

By the time he'd convinced Judy to come in immediately for closer monitoring, she was still calm and relatively relaxed, which considering her obstetric history was nothing short of a miracle.

If only *they* were as calm and relaxed things would be fine, but they weren't. Liv felt like a cat on hot bricks, and she wasn't sure he was faring any better.

They got through the morning by keeping out of each other's way as much as possible, avoiding eye contact, restricting conversation to a minimum and all work-related, but fun it wasn't and her nerves were in bits, so the second the clinic was finished she made her escape.

He closed the door as Liv went out with the last patient, leant back against the wall and closed his eyes, letting his breath out in a long, slow huff.

Well, they'd survived, if you could call it that.

Not that it had been easy, but they'd got through it by sticking to business and getting on with the job, and they'd done that well, working together as a smooth, well-oiled team just as they had in the old days. Except in the old days they'd enjoyed it, and he was pretty certain neither of them had enjoyed it today, and the tension between them could have been cut with a knife.

It couldn't go on like this, though, and he knew he had to do something to break through the icy politeness and careful distance between them or it wasn't going to work. At all.

He shrugged away from the wall, picked up the last set of notes and left the room, scanning the clinic for Liv, but there was no sign of her.

'Seen Liv?' he asked at Reception as he handed over the file, and was told she'd gone for lunch.

Which meant, unless she'd changed her habits, she'd be in the café that opened onto the park.

Good. He could do with a nice, strong coffee,

with caffeine in it for a change. It might help him get through what was sure to be a deeply awkward conversation.

CHAPTER TWO

'MIND IF I join you?'

She might have known he'd find her here. She should have gone to the other café, or the restaurant—or even better, gone off-site.

Too late now. She looked pointedly at the two free tables, then up into those beautiful, unreadable eyes that were studying her knowingly. Too knowingly. She looked away.

'Is this about work?'

'In a way.'

He didn't wait for her to invite him, just put his cup on the table and sat down, his gaze meeting hers again, but this time she didn't look away because his eyes looked guarded and a little wary still, and she realised he was—nervous? No, not nervous, that didn't sound like Nick. Uncomfortable, maybe. That didn't sound like him, either, not the Nick she knew and loved anyway, but maybe he'd changed. Maybe she'd changed him by cutting him so brutally out of her life, but she'd been so hurt...

'Liv, I realise this is awkward, but I do think we need to clear the air if we're going to work together,' he said quietly, 'unless you being in the clinic this morning was just a one-off?'

She shook her head. 'No, it wasn't a one-off, but I wasn't meant to be doing the clinic today and I didn't realise you'd be starting work so early. I thought it would take longer with HR.'

'Ah, well, that's the file for you,' he said with a slight smile that didn't reach his eyes. 'Answers all the questions in an instant. So, getting back to us, I'd assumed when Ben asked me that you'd still be in the midwife-led unit?'

She shook her head again. 'No, I only moved there while you were working your notice, and after you'd gone there was no point in me staying there, so I switched back to the consultant unit when there was a vacancy. I've been back six months.'

He frowned. 'I didn't know that. I'm sorry, I would have talked to you first if I had. Obviously I knew we'd see each other anyway from time to time, but that's not quite the same as having to work together. Are you going to be OK with that?'

Was she? OK with spending day after day bumping into him, working alongside him on deliveries, their hands, their bodies touching as they brushed against each other in the confines of the delivery room? OK with hearing his voice, catching endless glimpses of him around the maternity unit, hearing him laugh? He had a wonderful laugh, warm and rich and never, never unkind.

Would she really be OK with all of that?

She let out a soft, slightly shaky sigh. 'Nick, it's fine. We managed this morning and as I said to Ben, I'm sure we can be civilised.'

'I'm sure we can, but that still doesn't make it easy.'

The despairing little laugh escaped without her permission. 'What, you thought you could come back into my life after a year and it would be *easy*? Get real, Nick. We're not married any more, in case you hadn't noticed. Of course it won't be easy.'

He winced slightly—so slightly that anyone who didn't know him as well as she did wouldn't have spotted it, but when he spoke it was without emotion.

'We *are* still married,' he corrected, his voice carefully controlled, 'but I haven't forgotten for a single moment that we're not together. That's not what this is about. But we are going to have to work together, and we never had a problem in the past and I don't want us to have a problem now.'

'Did we have a problem today?'

'With the work? No. With the atmosphere, definitely, and I'm not sure I can do it unless we can find some middle ground. We used to be such a brilliant team, and I want to find a way to get that back.'

'Seriously?' she asked, slightly incredulous, but he nodded.

'Seriously. I realise it's not going to be the same, but it needs to be better than it was this morning, and I just wanted to clear the air, break the ice a bit and get rid of the awkwardness, so that we're more at ease next time.'

In his dreams. There was no way she was going to be at ease with him. She only had to hear his voice or catch a glimpse of him and her heart started racing, but he was here and she was stuck with it, for now at least, and he had a point. They did have to be able to work together, although she still had questions about that, so she went for the first one on the pile.

'How come you were available to locum anyway?' she asked without preamble. 'I'd imagined you tucked up in a nice little consultant's post somewhere picturesque.'

Probably with another woman. She didn't add that, because he was trying to pour oil on troubled waters and it wouldn't help at all if she threw petrol on the fire instead. And besides, it was none of her business any more who he chose to sleep with.

He glanced down, stirring his coffee on autopilot even though she knew it wouldn't have sugar in it.

'I didn't want to tie myself down,' he said, finally putting the spoon back in the saucer and meeting her eyes again. 'After I left here, I just wanted to get away, let the dust settle, work out where I wanted to go. I thought maybe New Zealand, but my parents are still alive and they're getting older, so I took a two-month locum post covering maternity leave fairly close to them while I worked out what I wanted to do, and then when that was coming to an end they asked me to cover the fertility clinic until it shut because the services were being centralised and the consultant had left, so I did. I saw my last patients two days ago, on the day Ben rang, and I had nothing else lined up, so I'm here.'

'Why on earth did you say yes?'

'To Ben? Because I need a job, so I can eat and keep a roof over both our heads.'

She felt another pang of guilt. 'I didn't mean that, Nick, but if the mortgage is an issue—'

'It's not an issue, Liv, it's a fact, and I'm not going to make you homeless under any circumstances so let's just ignore that. So what *did* you mean?'

'I was talking about the fertility clinic job. I couldn't believe it when Ben told me that's what you'd been doing. It seems such an odd choice to make, under the circumstances, and I couldn't understand why on earth you'd do it.'

His eyes flicked away, then back to hers, curiously intent. 'Because I needed a job, as I said, and I was already in the hospital, I'd made a few friends, it meant I wouldn't have to relocate—and maybe, also, because I thought it might help me understand what had happened to us.'

Her heart thumped. 'And did it?'

He smiled sadly. 'Well, let's just say it made it blindingly obvious that we weren't the only couple struggling.'

His expression wasn't guarded now, just full of regret, and she lowered her head, unable to hold those clear grey eyes that seemed to see to the bottom of her insecurities.

'How about you?' he asked softly. 'What have you been up to since I went?'

She picked up her spoon and chased the froth on her cappuccino, stalling just as he had. 'What I'm doing now, pretty much. What did you expect?'

'I didn't. I had no idea what you'd want to do.'

Cry? She'd done so much of that after he'd gone, but she wasn't telling him that, although he could probably work it out. Fix it? Impossible, because the thing that had been wrong was the thing they hadn't been able to fix, so she'd just got on with her life, putting one foot in front of the other, not even trying to make sense of it because there wasn't any sense to be made.

'I didn't want to do anything,' she said sadly, watching the froth slide off the spoon. 'I just wanted peace, that was all. Peace, contentment, and the satisfaction of a job well done instead of the endless spectre of failure—'

'You didn't fail, Liv!'

She dropped the spoon with a clatter. 'Really? So what would you call it? Month after month, all our hopes and dreams flushed away—and then, just to rub my nose in it, you go off and sleep with your ex. That doesn't exactly make it a success in my book—'

She pushed back her chair, grabbed her bag and walked swiftly away from him, out of the café into the park, hauling in the cold air as if she'd just come up from the bottom of the ocean.

Don't cry! Whatever you do, don't cry—

'Liv! Liv, wait!'

She turned and looked up at him, right behind her, his grey eyes troubled, and she had the crazy urge to throw herself into his arms and sob her heart out.

Don't cry!

'Leave it, Nick,' she said, hoping her voice didn't show her desperation. 'Just leave it. I don't mind working with you, I said that to Ben, and I'm sure we can keep it professional, but I don't need any cosy chats or in-depth analysis of where it all went wrong for us. We both know exactly where it all went wrong, and if I'd gone to the conference with you that weekend then you would never have slept with Suzanne—'

'I didn't sleep with her.'

She stared at him, stunned. *'What?'*

'I said, I didn't sleep with her.'

Shock robbed her of breath.

'I don't believe you. You're lying!'

'No, I'm not, Liv. I didn't touch her. Honestly.'

She took a step back, struggling for air, for sense, for understanding, but they all eluded her.

'That's not true. It can't be true. Why would you suddenly come out with this now?'

'Because it *is* true, and I should have told you at the time.'

How did he do that with his eyes? Make them appear utterly unguarded and shining with sincerity?

'But—you admitted it!'

'No. No, I didn't Liv, I just confirmed that she'd spent the night with me in my room,' he told her. 'That was what you asked me, and I said yes because it was the truth. She did spend the night in there with me. You didn't ask why, though, or what for, because by the time I came home you'd spoken to Beth, you'd found the note Suze had left in my luggage and you had me hung, drawn and quartered and hung out to dry before I even stepped over the threshold, so you wouldn't have believed me anyway.

'You just assumed I'd slept with her,' he went on, his voice heavy and tinged with sadness, 'and I let you, because in that split second I felt that you'd thrown me a lifeline, a way out of a marriage that was tearing us both apart, so I just grabbed it and ran. And I'm sorry. I should never have done that to you. I should have told you the truth there and then, and made you listen.'

His words stunned her, the shockwaves rolling through her, bringing a sob to her throat.

'How could you do that?' she asked, her voice a strangled whisper. 'How could you let me believe that for all this time? I've spent a whole, agonising year believing that you slept with her, that I wasn't enough for you, that you didn't truly love me any more—you're right, you should have told me the truth then, Nick, instead of letting me think that you'd spent the night making love to—'

She broke off, unable to say her name. 'You let me end our *marriage*, on the grounds that you'd slept with that *whore*—'

His eyes hardened. 'She's not a whore, she's a friend, a damn good friend, who told me to pull myself together and go home and sort out my marriage.'

A sob rose in her throat, threatening to choke her, but she crushed it down and pulled herself together. 'Well, you did a great job of that—'

Her voice cracked and she pushed past him, shaking his hand off as he tried to stop her. She went back inside, cutting through the café to the main hospital corridor, then out on the other side bordering the car park, deliberately going the wrong way to throw him off the scent and lose him because if she had to spend another moment in his company she was going to cry, and she wasn't prepared to give him the satisfaction.

So she kept on going, and she didn't stop until she was back on the ward.

She'd gone.

The corridor was empty and he stood there, kicking himself for letting the conversation stray into such dangerous territory—especially in a public place and right in the middle of the working day.

Idiot!

He had to talk to her, to explain why he'd let her believe what she had, how he'd felt, why he hadn't stood his ground and told her the truth at the time. The *real* reason.

But not now. This afternoon he had a—mercifully short—elective list, so his first port of call was the wards, to make sure Judy Richards was settled in, and to meet the patients he was going to operate on and read through their notes before he was due in Theatre. And if he was lucky, Liv's shift would be well and truly over by the time he'd finished.

He'd go and see her at home later, to apologise, to explain, to try and help her understand.

If he could get her to listen, and judging by the way she'd just reacted, that was by no means a foregone conclusion.

Liv was tied up in a delivery for the afternoon, the nice straightforward labour of a woman having her sixth baby. She'd haemorrhaged after the last so she'd been admitted directly to the consultant-led unit with this one just in case, but so far everything was going fine.

Just as well, because Liv's concentration was totally shot.

How could he have done that to her? Let her believe he'd betrayed her like that if he hadn't? And why then, when she'd just found out that *yet again* she wasn't pregnant, so she'd been at her most vulnerable? She'd spent over a year living with the bone-deep certainty that he'd been unfaithful to her, and now she didn't know what to believe—

'I need to push.'

'OK, Karen. Nice and steady. That's good.'

But Karen's baby wasn't going for nice and steady, and three minutes later, half an hour before the end of Liv's shift, a lusty, squalling baby was delivered into her father's waiting hands.

'It's a girl,' he said, laughing and crying as he lay their daughter in his wife Karen's outstretched arms. 'Finally, it's a girl!'

Liv's eyes filled, and she had to blink away the tears as she gave Karen the oxytocin injection to help her uterus to contract down.

If this had been them, if she'd been able to give him a child, then maybe that would have been enough to keep him...

Liv checked the baby quickly as she lay in her mother's arms, making sure that all was well, but the baby was lovely and pink, her pulse steady and strong, her skinny little arms and legs moving beautifully. She'd stopped crying now and was staring up at her mother, riveted by the first face she'd ever seen.

It was a beautiful moment, one Liv never tired of seeing, and she watched the two of them staring into each other's eyes and falling in love and felt a familiar lump in her throat.

'Apgar score ten at one minute,' she said, her voice miraculously steady. 'Congratulations. She's lovely.'

She checked her again four minutes later, by which time the cord had stopped pulsating, so Liv clamped and cut it and handed the baby back to her mother.

'I take it this is your first girl?'

Her father's grin was wry. 'Yes, so hopefully we can stop now. Six is getting a little crazy, but we did want a girl so we thought we'd have one last try.'

'We may live to regret it when she hits puberty,' Karen said with a laugh, her hands cradling the naked baby tenderly at her breast.

Liv laid a warm towel back over them both and tucked it round the baby. 'She'll be fine, and she'll have all those big brothers to look after her. She's latched on well,' Liv added, struck yet again by the miracle of birth and the naturalness of this wonderful bond between mother and child. The bond she would never know...

'Yes, and thank goodness I've never had any problems with feeding any of them,' Karen said with a laugh. 'There's way too much to do in our house without sterilising bottles and making up feeds. Ooh, I can feel a contraction.'

'OK, Karen, that's good, you're nearly done.

Gentle push for me when you're ready?' she said calmly, but Liv felt her heart rate pick up, because this was the moment, as the placenta separated from the uterine wall, that the haemorrhage would happen, and she really, really didn't feel ready for that.

Didn't feel ready for any more stress today, and the last thing she needed was Nick striding in there to take over like the cavalry after he'd just destabilised her fragile status quo with that bombshell about Suzanne.

Concentrate!

The haemorrhage didn't happen. To everyone's huge relief, the placenta came away cleanly with hardly any blood loss, so after they'd sorted Karen out and Liv was happy that her uterus was contracting down well and that all was as it should be, she left the other midwife to fill out the notes and headed for the changing room, only an hour late.

Tomorrow was Saturday, and with any luck she wouldn't run into Nick again today which meant she was unlikely to see him again until Monday. That would give her two clear days to get her emotions in order.

Except it didn't, because she walked out of the lift at the bottom of the building and ran slap into him.

'Sorry—'

She stepped hastily back, and they stood trans-fixed in awkward silence as the lift doors hissed shut behind her, cutting off her retreat.

'I gather your delivery was all right?' he asked, breaking the silence. 'I've been on standby in case she haemorrhaged again.'

'Oh—yes, it was fine, thanks. No problems. How's Judy Richards?'

'Settling in. I think I've reassured her.' He paused, his eyes searching hers. 'Look, Liv, are you done for the day?'

'Yes,' she said firmly, holding his eyes with a determined effort and clutching her coat in her arms like a shield. 'And I'm going home.'

'Can we talk?'

Her heart sank. 'Again? Nick, there's nothing you have to say that I need to hear. If there's a shred of truth in what you said, you should have told me then, not saved it for now, and I really don't want to discuss it. For heaven's sake, just leave it. It's not relevant any more anyway.'

She pushed past him and walked out of the door, but of course he couldn't leave it, could he? She could barely hear his footsteps behind her but she knew he was there, his voice calling her name as she made her way across the car park, but it was almost drowned out by the pounding of her heart.

She dodged between the rows of cars, reached the kerb by the access road to the main car park and was about to cross it when she felt his hand on her arm.

'Liv, please, let me talk to you. Give me a chance to explain.'

But she'd had enough to deal with already today, so she turned back to face him and shook her head. 'No. I can't do this now just to ease your guilty conscience, Nick, and I'm not going to. Please, just leave me alone!'

He caught her shoulders and held her. 'Liv, I won't take much of your time, but there's something I need to tell you and you need to hear it—'

'No! No, I don't!'

She tried to spin away from him, but his grip suddenly tightened and he tried to pull her back.

'Liv, no!' he yelled, his voice urgent, but the

urgency was lost on her as she wrenched her arm away and stumbled backwards off the kerb out of reach.

She saw the look of horror on his face, heard the blast of a horn, saw the car as it clipped her and sent her spinning, and then her head hit the ground and everything went black…

He watched helplessly as the car struck her, saw her fall, saw her head bouncing off the kerb as she came to rest just inches from the front wheel. The big SUV had ground to a halt and the driver stumbled out, other people ran towards them shouting, but his eyes were only for Liv.

She was lying motionless on the edge of the road like a broken doll, her head level with the front wheel, her feet partly under the car just inches from the rear wheel, and for a terrifying second he thought she was dead.

Her hair had tumbled over her face and he dropped to his knees beside her, sweeping the hair aside to check for a pulse in her neck, but his own heart was beating so hard he could scarcely feel hers and his breath jammed in his throat.

'Liv? Liv, talk to me, for God's sake!'

He found a pulse and dragged in a breath, digging out the doctor instead of the lover, running his hands over her quickly, checking that she was breathing, scanning her for injuries, but her limbs were all straight, her pupils were equal and reactive, her breathing was normal. For now. But she was unconscious, and that could mean anything.

He needed help, and fast. He tugged his phone out of his pocket with shaking fingers and rang the ED direct. 'One of our midwives has been knocked down near the staff car park and she's unconscious. Send a team out here now, please, fast. Tell them they'll need a collar and board and a pelvic band. And hurry.'

She started to stir, and he dropped the phone and reached out, bracketing her head carefully in his hands and holding it steady, feeling the stickiness of blood on his fingers as they burrowed through her hair. No…

'Easy, Liv. Try not to move. I've called for help. Just stay as still as you can.'

'Nick?'

She knew him. Thank God…

'It's OK, Liv, I've got you, my love. I've got

you. They'll be here soon. You'll be OK. Just keep still for me, sweetheart.'

'My head hurts…'

'I know, darling, I know, but they'll be here soon. Just hang on another minute. It won't be long.'

'Over here,' someone yelled, and then the crowd that had gathered around them parted as the trauma team arrived.

He looked up without moving his hands. 'She was KOed briefly, she's got a head wound, and you'll need a collar and a board. GCS three at first, now fourteen. She's concussed, almost certainly whiplashed and she could have pelvic and spinal injuries—and mind her legs. I don't know if they were hit,' he said unsteadily, and then someone took over the control of her head and neck and he found himself gently shifted out of the way. Someone backed the car away very carefully to give them better access, and as soon as her spine was immobilised they moved her onto a stretcher, then up onto the trolley for the short trundle to the ED doors.

He scooped up her bag and coat and went with them, still issuing instructions on autopilot. 'Try and keep it smooth,' he said, putting his free hand on the trolley to steady it. 'She'll need a head and neck CT and a full trauma series—'

'It's OK, you can leave her with us now,' someone said, but he shook his head.

'No way, she's my wife,' he said, for the sake of economy, and he followed them into Resus without waiting to be invited. The team closed around her, nobody he recognised, no one he could connect with, and then a door swished open and someone said, 'OK, what have we got?' and the voice from his youth was so familiar he could have cried with relief.

'Sam,' he said, his voice choked, and Sam stopped in his tracks and did a mild double-take.

'Nick? What are you doing here?'

'My wife was knocked down in the car park, right in front of me. Her name's Olivia—Liv. She's a midwife here.'

'Liv's your wife?' Sam's face creased into a frown and he bent over her so she could see his face without moving. 'Hi, Liv, it's Sam Ryder. Remember me? You delivered our baby last year.'

'Of course I do. How is she?' she mumbled,

and Nick let out a sigh of relief because if she remembered that, it was a good sign—wasn't it?

'She's fine. They're both well.' Sam turned to him. 'What can you tell me about the accident? Speed, angle of collision, how far she travelled?'

He made himself focus. 'Um—low speed collision, probably less than ten miles an hour at the most? She stepped out backwards in front of a big SUV. She was hit from her left side and spun as she fell, but not far. Her head hit the kerb pretty hard. There's a cut on the left side just behind the temple. GCS three initially, then fourteen after a brief loss of consciousness—'

'How brief?'

He shrugged. 'I don't know. Not long, but long enough to be significant. A minute, maybe, at the most? I'd done a cursory check and called for help before she stirred.'

'Did her head hit the bonnet before she fell?'

'No. No, it really wasn't that fast and the front wing just clipped her. She just—spun and fell, but really hard so she'll need a CT and her head's bleeding so she could have a fracture there where she hit the kerb, and she might be whiplashed and her spine needs checking thoroughly—'

Sam lifted a hand. 'OK, we're on it. Can you give us her details so we can be getting her notes up? And then maybe you need to go and get a coffee while we check her over.'

'I can't leave her—'

'Yes, you can. Don't worry, we'll keep you updated. Make sure we've got your number.'

Sam turned back to Liv, taking her hand in his, focusing intently on his patient as Nick stood numbly and watched them, hardly daring to breathe.

'OK, Liv, can you tell me where it hurts?' Sam asked softly.

'Everywhere.'

'Well, that's not very useful,' he said with a grin. 'Can you try and be a little more specific?'

'My head?'

'Anywhere else?' He carried on chattily assessing her while Nick watched tensely from the sidelines, then he straightened.

'OK. That's all good. Can we get some IV paracetamol on board, please, and get a full trauma screen to rule out any fractures and then we'll send you down for a head and neck CT,

Liv, OK? And can we run a FAST scan, please, while we're waiting?'

Nick felt himself relax a fraction. Despite his light-hearted banter, Sam was looking after her properly, and all the time the nurses had been working, linking her to a monitor, getting IV access ready, cutting her clothes away so Sam could see her injuries.

He could see them, too, and the bruises on her smooth, pale skin made him wince. She could so easily have been killed—

'Mr Jarvis?'

He turned his head, finally becoming aware of the nurse who'd laid a hand on his arm and was shaking it gently to get his attention.

'If you could give me her details that would be very helpful.'

'Of course. I'm sorry.' He forced himself to focus, rattled off her name, date of birth, address, GP—

'OK, I've got her. You're her next of kin?'

'Yes,' he said firmly, although he didn't know if that was still true, strictly speaking, because the ex-ness made that all a little unclear…

'Same mobile phone number?'

'Yes.'

'Is that her stuff? Would you like me to look after it?'

He looked down and saw the coat and bag, clutched in his hand like a lifeline. He'd forgotten all about them. 'Yeah, thanks.' He handed them over just as the door behind him opened again and swished shut, and he turned his head and met Ben Walker's worried eyes.

'What's going on? I heard Liv had been run over.'

'Not run over,' he said, his voice suddenly hollow. 'She was knocked down. She's got a head injury.'

Ben frowned, crossed over to the bed and exchanged a few words with Sam, then leant over her. 'Hi, Liv. Anything I can do?'

She mumbled something, and Ben nodded and straightened up, squeezing her hand as he left her side.

'Don't worry, I'll look after him.'

He turned to the nurse who was printing up Liv's labels for the notes. 'Page me if you need us,' he said, and hooking his arm around Nick's shoulders, the bluff Yorkshireman gently but firmly led him away.

CHAPTER THREE

BEN STEERED HIM through the department and out of the doors on the park side of the building.

The cold March air hit him, and he hauled in a breath and gagged.

'I feel sick,' he said, and doubled over, retching emptily.

He felt Ben's hand on his back. 'Come on. We'll find a bench where you can sit down and I'll go and get us a drink.'

He nodded and straightened up, following Ben obediently across the grass on legs that weren't quite steady. 'I thought she was dead, Ben. She was about to step out in front of this massive SUV, right in front of my eyes, and I tried to hold her but she pulled away and fell backwards and it smacked into her and then she was lying there, so still, her feet just inches from the wheels—'

'Nick, she's alive and conscious and talking, and Sam will be doing everything he can to make sure she stays that way. Now sit down before you fall down.'

They'd reached a bench, and he didn't need telling twice. He dropped onto it and propped his elbows on his knees, trying to slow his breathing and regain control of his emotions. After a few seconds he straightened up and glanced across at Ben, who was sitting beside him watching him thoughtfully.

'Better?'

He nodded. 'Yeah. Sorry.'

The hand on his shoulder was warm and firm and comforting. 'Don't be. You're in shock, and I'd be just the same if it was Daisy or one of the kids. How do you take your tea?'

'Coffee, for a start, black, no sugar—and if you put a ton of sugar in it, I'll pour it on the grass, so don't even try.'

Ben grunted and got to his feet without bothering to comment. 'Have you eaten today?'

'Not since seven. I didn't manage to get lunch.'

Too busy trashing what was left of his relationship with Liv...

'Right. I'll get you something to eat, as well. Stay here.'

He didn't think he had a choice. He was seriously unsure his legs would hold him if he tried to get up, and he swallowed on another wave of nausea.

Shock, he realised numbly. He was in shock, as Ben had said, but Liv was alive, Sam was looking after her and if he was as good a doctor as he was a sailor, she was in safe hands.

All he could do was wait.

So this is what it's like in a scanner, she thought, but she felt curiously detached, as if it wasn't really happening to her.

It didn't take long, and then she was wheeled back to the ED, lying on her back staring at the ceiling as it whizzed past and feeling disorientated. She knew the route well, but she'd never seen it from this angle. Weird.

They went through several sets of doors, and came to rest at last in Resus. She was glad they'd stopped. Her head was spinning and even the slight jiggle of the trolley along the smooth corridors had made it hurt more.

'OK?' Sam asked, smiling down at her, and

she tried to smile back but it felt like a pretty poor effort and she just wanted Nick.

'I think so. My head aches a bit.'

'It will. You've had quite a bump, Liv, but nothing's broken and there's no evidence of a brain injury. You might be pretty sore for a while, though, but your spine's OK and so's your pelvis, so we can get rid of all this stuff and someone'll come and clean you up a bit and then I'll get you moved out of Resus.'

'What happened to my clothes? I don't remember anyone taking them off.'

'We cut them off you,' he said, frowning slightly. 'When you were brought in.'

'Oh.' She thought hard, but came up with nothing. 'I didn't register that. I suppose you had to. Where's Nick?'

'I don't know, but when I find him he's going to ask me questions and I gather from Ben that you're not together any more, so do I have your permission to talk to him about your results, or would you rather I didn't?'

Her results? 'Yes—yes, of course. If you don't tell him he'll only ask me anyway so you might as well.'

Sam chuckled. 'That sounds like him. OK, I'll go and find him while we get you sorted. He won't be far away.'

He was in the relatives' room where Ben had left him when Sam came in. He tried to get up, but Sam put a hand on his shoulder and pushed him gently back down. It wasn't hard. His legs felt like jelly and he thought he was going to be sick again.

He opened his mouth to ask how she was, but he didn't need to, Sam got there before him.

'She's OK, Nick. She's doing all right.'

He let his breath out in a rush and crushed the sudden urge to cry. 'No brain injury?'

Sam sat down beside him and shook his head.

'No. Not as far as we can see but we'll watch that. Her CT was clear, her X-rays didn't reveal any fractures, but she's got a small cut on her scalp which I'm going to glue, and she's going to have some colourful bruises. There's the odd superficial graze from contact with the ground, of course, and she's going to be sore, but all in all she's got away with it pretty lightly. Assuming there's no silent head injury waiting to show itself, she should be fine in a day or so but she might be a bit concussed. She's got a headache, so I want to keep an eye on that, but it's probably a bit of whiplash.'

He nodded, swallowing. 'Can I see her now?'

'In a minute. I'll get someone to take you to her as soon as she's ready. I'm going to keep her on fifteen-minute obs for a while, and I'm probably going to admit her overnight, just in case. She didn't seem to remember we'd cut her clothes off, but that might just be shock. She was still in the neck brace so she might not even have realised what we were doing, but I don't want to make assumptions and miss anything.'

Nick tried to smile. 'Don't worry, I won't let you. I'll be right there by her side and I'll be watching her like a hawk.'

'Good. I'll let you know when she's ready. Oh, and the police want to talk to you about the accident. I'll get them to come and see you now. Don't move.'

It seemed to take an age before the police were finished with him, but finally he was able to go and see Liv. She was in a bed in the small observation ward, her lashes dark against her pale cheeks, and she looked so frail and vulnerable that his heart wrenched. It could so easily have been so much worse. It might yet be…

The chair creaked as he sat down, and her lids fluttered open and her head turned towards him.

'Nick?'

He stood up and moved to her side, gripping the cot sides on the edge of the bed as he stared down at her ashen face. A bruise was coming out on her cheekbone, blue against the pale skin, and he swallowed hard. 'Yes, it's me, Liv. Is that OK, or do you want me to leave?'

'No, stay with me, please?' Her hand fluttered, and he reached down and slipped his fingers through hers and they curled around his and clung.

'How are you feeling?' he asked, aware of how gruff his voice sounded but unable to do anything about it.

She shrugged slightly, and winced. 'Sore?' she said, sounding weak and tired and nothing like his Liv. 'I've got a banging headache and everything's feeling a bit tender. Sam said I was lucky not to break anything, but it doesn't feel lucky from where I'm lying.'

'It's lucky,' he said fervently. 'Trust me, it's lucky. I watched that car hit you, and for a minute there—well, whatever. If I hadn't followed you—'

'Nick, it wasn't your fault I stepped out in front of it.'

'Don't, Liv. I don't want to think about it. It's all I can see as it is, and it *was* my fault, I should have listened to you and let you go.' He lifted her hand to his mouth and pressed a long, lingering kiss to the back of her fingers. 'Is there anything I can do for you, anything I can get you?'

'A taxi?' she joked weakly. 'Not that I can go anywhere. They cut my clothes off.'

He frowned. 'They had to, Liv. They had no idea what injuries you had, and anyway, hitting the tarmac won't have done them any good. And as for the taxi, you're going nowhere,' he said firmly. 'Sam's talking about admitting you overnight for observation and I think it's a good idea.'

'No-o. I don't want to stay in,' she moaned softly. 'It's so noisy here. I just want my own bed.'

'OK. Maybe later. I'll talk to Sam,' he murmured to stall her, although he knew darned well what Sam would say, and so, apparently, did she.

'My parents used to do that,' she said, her voice tailing off. 'I'll ask your father. I'll see what your mother says. All stalling tactics. The answer never did change...'

Her lids drifted down, her lashes coming to rest against her bleached skin, and as her hand relaxed he laid it down gently, let his breath out on a slow, silent huff and lowered himself onto the chair again, never taking his eyes off her.

She'd get better a lot quicker, Liv thought, if they'd only leave her alone to sleep, but she knew why they were doing it, and it was reassuring in a mildly irritating way.

The nurses came intermittently to do her obs, and after a while Nick told them not to bother, he'd do them. It meant he had to touch her, to feel the pulse beating in her wrist, to check her pupils with a pen light, and although he was doing exactly what the nurses had, somehow his touch was different.

Not quite so clinical as theirs, lingering a little

longer than was strictly necessary, and his voice was quiet and soothing but also filled with an emotion that he either didn't or couldn't disguise. And when she had to stare into his eyes so he could test her pupil reflexes, there was a tenderness there that made her want to cry.

A nurse brought him a cup of tea at one point, and a couple of times Sam popped his head round the curtain, glanced at her chart and exchanged a few words with them, asked her questions, made her squeeze his hands, push against him, wiggle her toes, shone a light in her eyes to check her pupil reflexes and accommodation, but all of it with an appropriate clinical detachment which just made Nick's touch all the more obviously different.

It was weird having him there with her. He was so gentle, so quiet and unobtrusive, and yet even when he was sitting silently beside her, she was aware of him with every battered cell in her body. She'd been so desperate to get away from him that she'd nearly died, and now that seemed ridiculous because she actually wanted him there, crazy though it was.

Because she still loved him, despite the lie?

Maybe even *because* of it—because of the fact that he hadn't, after all, slept with Suzanne.

Why not? She wouldn't have blamed him—or Suze, come to that. She was a beautiful woman, and he was a beautiful man. Why wouldn't they want each other? It wasn't as if it would have been the first time—and it wasn't as if things had been exactly peachy in the months leading up to it, and that was her own fault as much as his.

She'd spent the last year blaming herself for shutting him out and driving him to it, but he'd shut her out, too, and their relationship had been crumbling for months before it had reached crisis point.

He was right, they did need to talk, but not now, and not here, in probably the busiest department of the hospital. Now, with her head hurting and every part of her starting to ache, all she wanted was to go home.

Sam, though, had other ideas. Before he'd discuss it he wanted a urine sample to check for blood, presumably to see if she'd sustained kidney damage.

'I'll get a bedpan,' Nick said, but she was ready for that and dismissed it instantly.

'No way. Or a commode. The loo—as in proper plumbing, running water, and a door that shuts.'

'I don't think—'

'Good. Don't bother,' she said, trying to sound firm and failing miserably. 'Seriously, Nick, if you won't let me walk, then get me a wheelchair, and if you won't do that then I'll crawl on my hands and knees. Please don't make me, because I will do it.' Her voice cracked, and she bit her lips and waited.

She watched his internal battle, and then to her relief he sighed quietly and got to his feet. 'Still as stubborn as ever, then,' he said mildly, and went, presumably to find a wheelchair.

'Going somewhere?' Sam asked as Nick wheeled it in.

'Yeah. It has to be the loo, apparently.'

'Well, stay with her.'

'I will.'

'Over my dead body,' she said, and Sam just laughed, but Nick frowned, his face a mask.

'Can we not talk about your dead body, please?'

he said tightly, and she felt a chill run over her. If that car had been going a little quicker, she might not be here now. There'd been a fraction of a second when everything had gone into slow motion, and she'd been sure she was going to die. What must it have been like for him to watch it all happen and be unable to prevent it? To feel that he'd caused it, even?

Horrendous, and it was only by the grace of God that she wasn't dead or far more critically injured. No wonder he was fussing over her. After all, he'd loved her once, and maybe, in a way, still did. And despite their problems, he was a good man. Way too good to have deserved the way she'd treated him.

'Sorry,' she said soberly, cutting him some slack. 'If you could just wheel me there, please, I can do the rest.'

He had an opinion, of course, but in the end she won and he hovered outside the door until she'd finished and then took the urine sample off her and wheeled her back to bed.

'OK?' he asked as she sank back against the pillows with relief.

'Mmm. Thanks. Could you give that to Sam and ask him when I can go home?'

'You can ask me yourself,' Sam said, appearing at the foot of the bed and giving her a wry smile. 'You won't like the answer.'

'Oh, no, Sam, really? I'm fine—'

'No, you're not, Liv,' Sam told her gently. 'You're doing OK, but you're not fine, and if you've got a silent head injury—'

'Then I'll call someone.'

'Not if you can't,' Nick growled from beside her. 'You need monitoring all night.'

'No, I don't! I'm fine, Nick, and if you won't discharge me, Sam, I'm going to discharge myself.'

'Liv, I really—'

'No, Nick! This is none of your business. I appreciate your concern, both of you, but I don't want to stay in. I've got a few bruises—'

'You were out cold!'

'For seconds—'

'It still counts, Liv,' Sam interjected, but she just glared at him.

'I. Want. To. Go. Home,' she said, stressing every word as if she was talking to a pair of idiots, which frankly she felt she was. Her head was killing her, everything hurt and she just wanted out. Now. Before she broke down and let out all the emotions that were building inside her.

Sam looked at her, looked at Nick and looked back at her again—and gave in.

'OK,' he said, to her astonishment. 'On one condition.'

'Anything,' she said rashly.

'Nick stays with you.'

'No!'

They spoke together, but Sam just arched a brow and shrugged. 'Your choice. It's that or nothing.'

'I'll discharge myself.'

Nick felt sick again. She would, he knew that. The woman was stubborn enough for anything, even if it worked against her. He'd learned that years ago, and he'd given up fighting it.

But this was different. This was her life they were talking about, and her safety was more important to him than anything else and he'd done enough to compromise it today already.

'I'll do it,' he said. 'If you insist on going home, I'll do it.'

'No. It's not necessary.'

'Take it or leave it, Liv,' he said flatly. 'Either I'm there with you, or you're here, which is definitely my preferred option.'

'It's not your option to have, and you can't make me—'

'Watch me. I've already seen you nearly get killed once today because of me. I won't stand back and watch you have another go. As I said, take it or leave it, but that's the way it is.'

She frowned, lifting her hand to her head and pressing it against her forehead as if she was trying to push away the pain. Finally her arm dropped in a gesture of defeat.

'OK. You win. Come home with me if you think you have to, but it's totally unnecessary and I'm not happy about it.'

'Tough. At least I'll be able to live with myself,' he told her.

Sam rolled his eyes and grinned. 'Right. Now that's sorted, I'll go check this urine for blood, and if it's OK I'll authorise your discharge so that we can all go home tonight,' he said, and Nick watched her close her eyes with a sigh.

'I'm still not happy,' she grumbled, but he wasn't going to argue. He'd won this round. For now, that was enough.

It was almost ten that night before he pulled up on the drive of the home they'd shared for three years.

When they'd bought it just over four years ago, a bright future lay ahead of them. Little had they known how it was all going to pan out, but those happy days—and nights—now seemed a lifetime ago and he'd almost forgotten what home meant.

'Keys?' he said to her, and she rummaged in her bag and held them out to him.

'The burglar alarm's set. My code's 0901—and there's a mortice lock on the door now, too.'

The security lights triggered as he got out of the car, which was just as well, as he had to find the new keyhole.

Why the new lock? To stop him getting back in? And changing the code? She hadn't needed to do that. She should have known he wouldn't have invaded her privacy. Maybe he should have done, should have stuck it out and had the rest of the conversation she'd cut off at the ankles when she'd thrown him out, and maybe then he'd still have been with her, instead of drifting around in limbo and living alone in a box no bigger than their double garage.

He let out a tired sigh and swung the door open, stepping into the hall with a curious sense of déjà vu. He didn't know what he'd expected— that she would have changed the decor, or moved the furniture—anything, really, apart from nothing, which was what confronted him.

The same colour walls—not quite white, a soft touch of earthy grey taking the edge off it—the same striped stair carpet in muted greys and neutrals, the chair that sat randomly in the corner for no apparent reason—even the basket of carefully pressed and folded washing on the third step waiting for her to make a journey upstairs and take it with her.

It could have sat there untouched since the day she'd thrown him out—on the ninth of January. Hence the code for the burglar alarm, he realised belatedly.

Swallowing the lump in his throat, he turned it off ran upstairs with the washing basket and put it on the floor in their—correction, *her*—bedroom, and ran back down to help her out of the car.

Too slow.

'Liv, what are you doing?'

She lifted her head and frowned at him. 'What do you think I'm doing?' she asked, levering herself to her feet. 'It's obvious.'

Stubborn woman. 'Here, let me help you—'

Her level stare stopped him in his tracks, her pride obviously overriding common sense. 'Nick, relax, I can manage. You're only here because Sam insisted. I don't *need* you to help me.'

Which would have been fine, had she not then swayed against the car and let out a stifled groan.

He didn't wait to be asked. She'd be on the floor before she admitted she needed him for anything at all, so he just stepped in, laid her right arm carefully over his shoulders and put his other arm around her waist to steady her.

'Headrush?' he asked quietly, and she nodded.

'Mmm. It's OK now.' But she didn't try and shake him off, which she would have done if she'd truly been OK, so he walked her carefully to the front door, helped her over the doorstep, and then lowered her gently to the chair. He'd never seen the point of it until now, he thought wryly, watching as she sat silently on it with her eyes shut and a tiny frown creasing her brow.

The bruise on her cheekbone was spreading, coming out nicely in a black and blue stain that extended up into her hair and round the edge of her eye, steadily creeping across her eyebrow and down onto the lid. The only reason her face wasn't scraped was that her thick, dark hair had tumbled across her cheek and protected it as she'd hit the tarmac, and it had been further back on the side of her head that she'd taken the brunt of the fall. Hence the dried blood matted in her hair—

Her eyes opened again and she lifted her head and looked at him, the frown deepening. 'What?'

'What do you mean, what?'

'You were looking at me funny. You still are.'

He clenched his teeth, swallowing the horror he'd been reliving, the sight of her crashing to the ground, the way her head had bounced off the kerb—

'You're imagining it,' he said dismissively. 'Where to? Up or down?'

She looked at the stairs, her eyes running up the flight as if to assess the enormity of the task, then back to him as the fight went out of her. 'It all looks like too much effort but I suppose I really ought to go to bed before I can't get there.'

'Is there anything I can do to help you?'

She shook her head. 'No. I'll manage, Nick.'

She shrugged off her coat, took a deep breath and tackled the stairs. They seemed endless but she made it, only because she didn't really have a choice if she was going to be comfortable, but her head was pounding and she felt dizzy halfway up and had to lean on him.

'Just a few more steps to go,' Nick murmured, his warm, solid body reassuringly close behind her, and she gritted her teeth and made it up the last ones, pausing to lean on him for another moment before tackling the short distance across the landing to the bed.

He flicked back the covers, and she sat down gingerly on the edge with a sigh of relief, cold sweat beading on her forehead.

'OK?'

'Yes, I'm OK. I'm up here anyway. Maybe I should have some painkillers. My head's banging like a drum now.'

'Maybe you should. Let's get you comfy and I'll sort you out a drink to take them with.'

He shifted the pillows, stacking them up so she could lean back on them while she kicked off her shoes and then swung her legs up.

'Oh, that's better.' She sighed, settling against the pillows. 'I just feel a bit battered all over, and my head aches. I keep telling it I feel better, but it hasn't got the memo yet.'

He gave a wry huff of laughter, and he ran downstairs and brought her back a glass of water to take the paracetamol.

'Have you had any other drugs today? Any other pain relief?'

'No, I haven't. You know I don't take drugs. Only the IV paracetamol they gave me this afternoon, and that was hours ago. Just give it to me, for heaven's sake, and don't fuss.'

'I wouldn't dream of it,' he said drily, handing her the water and holding out his hand with the pills in.

She took them, washed them down with water

and handed the glass back with an apologetic sigh. 'Thank you. I'm sorry I've been so bitchy. I just…'

'Forget it,' he said softly. 'Tea? Coffee? Something to eat?'

'Tea would be lovely. And some toast, maybe? I'm starving. I don't know what happened to lunch.'

He did. He'd messed it up, like he'd messed so many things up. He put the glass on the bedside table and went back down to the kitchen. It hadn't changed any more than the rest, and he glanced across to the family room, his eyes settling on the sofa where it had all unravelled.

It could have been yesterday, he thought, if it wasn't for the wrenching heartache that had filled every day since she'd told him she wanted a divorce—a divorce that had never happened, for some reason.

He rested his hands on the edge of the worktop, hung his head and let out a shaky sigh. He so hadn't wanted to do this, to be here with her in this way, forced together by circumstances and Sam's well-meant interference, but he was the best candidate for the job.

He knew every inch of the house, could find his way round the kitchen in the dark, and, more importantly, knew Liv well enough to override her when necessary. That didn't mean he was going to enjoy it, and he knew it wouldn't be easy, not if she had anything to say about it—and he was sure she would, in spades.

Oh, well. One thing at a time.

He straightened up, hauled in a bracing lungful of air and put the kettle on.

CHAPTER FOUR

'DOES BEN KNOW you're not staying there to-night?'

He glanced up at her, taking his eyes off the midwifery journal he'd been pretending to read. As if she hadn't realised that. He hadn't turned a page in the last few minutes and his face had been like a frozen mask.

'Yes. I rang him just before we left the hospital. He's been fretting about you. He took me for coffee and force-fed me a disgustingly sweet chocolate muffin when Sam kicked me out of Resus, but then he had to go back to work. He's been bombarding me with texts ever since, asking how you are.'

She laughed softly and then winced, and he frowned.

'You OK?'

She nodded. 'My stomach muscles hurt a bit.

I guess being flung around like that'd cause all sorts of odd aches and pains.'

He frowned again at that, no doubt reliving the accident, and she regretted mentioning it.

'You probably tensed up to protect yourself. Are the painkillers working yet?'

She would have laughed under normal circumstances, but she'd tried that once. 'Not so you'd notice,' she told him. 'I need to get out of this lot,' she said, plucking at the horrible hospital gown and the borrowed scrub bottoms they'd lent her in the ED.

'Really? I thought it was rather fetching. The little NHS logo all over the gown goes really well with your eyes, but it's your choice.'

'Good of you to remember that,' she said drily. 'There's a long pink T-shirt with short sleeves in the second drawer, on the left.'

'Do you really need it?'

He sounded puzzled, and she forced herself to look up and meet his eyes. 'Yes, I do, because you're going to be here and we're not together any more,' she told him bluntly.

He rolled his eyes. 'Jeez, Liv, give me credit. I just thought you'll be more comfortable with nothing on. I'm hardly going to take advantage of it.'

'It's nothing to do with that,' she said, remembering when he'd taken every opportunity to do exactly that, but that was a long time ago, well before she'd thrown him out. Their problems had started long before then. She sighed. So much water under so many bridges…

'Nick, I can't be bothered to argue,' she told him. 'Just find it, please, could you, and then leave me alone? The bathroom's just here, not ten feet from the bed. I'll be fine.'

That sounded churlish, and she didn't mean it to. She let out a shaky sigh and shook her head. 'Sorry. That came out all wrong but I'm too tired to play games and I just want to go to sleep.'

She looked up at him, and saw sorrow etched on his face.

'It's OK, Liv. I understand,' he said softly. 'I know you don't want me here, but it's not for long. You'll be fine in a day or two.'

He was wrong. She did want him there, but not like this. Not shackled by duty and guilt, but there because he loved her.

He found the T-shirt, put it on the bed beside her and went out of the room. Not far, she knew that from the creaks on the landing, but far enough. He was probably sitting on the top step. She swung her legs over the side of the bed as she sat up, then unfastened the hideous hospital gown and tried to peel it off her shoulders, but they protested and she stifled a whimper.

Come on, girl, toughen up.

She got there in the end and pulled the long top on, then stood up, but as she bent over to push the trousers down she felt her head start to swim again.

She let out a little wail of frustration as she sagged back onto the bed, and the door swung open and Nick walked in.

'Feel free to knock,' she grumbled, but he ignored it and crouched down in front of her, his hands resting lightly on her knees as he looked up at her.

'What happened?' he asked gently. 'Another headrush?'

'Mmm. My head started swimming again when I bent over to take the scrubs off.'

'I'm not surprised, you've got concussion,' he said, easing them off over her feet as his eyes scanned the bruises that were coming out on her legs. His voice was calm, but she was sure he didn't feel calm. She could see the pulse beating in his throat as he looked at the bruises, and she knew he was holding his feelings in. Maybe it was just as well. She was on the brink of losing it as it was, and if he'd been nice to her, shown the slightest sign of caring, she would have crumpled like a wet tissue. Might anyway...

He stood up. 'Let me check your obs again,' he said, all business now suddenly, as if that was the easiest way to cope. He probably wasn't wrong.

He took the pen light he'd raided off Sam out of his pocket and turned it on, crouching down in front of her again. 'OK, look at me,' he said, and flashed it in her eyes in turn while she stared straight back into his. He had such beautiful eyes, and there'd been a time not so very long ago when they'd looked at her lovingly. Now, it was all business.

'OK, follow the pen.'

She followed it dutifully, overwhelmingly conscious of his left hand on the edge of the bed close to her right hip, steadying himself as he balanced on the balls of his feet. He was so close to her that she could feel the warmth coming off his body, smell the faint and yet unmistakable scent that was uniquely him.

She'd missed that, missed snuggling up to him, missed his arms around her, his heart beating under her ear—

'OK, your eyes are fine. Squeeze my hands?'

His grip was sure but gentle, and after she'd squeezed and relaxed he let her fingers lie in his. Only for a moment, but longer than was strictly necessary, then he let them go and stood up briskly, and she felt cool air sweep in where his warmth had been.

'You'll do,' he said, his voice suddenly gruff.

'I could have told you that. I need the loo now.'

'Can you manage on your own or do you need my help?'

'No, I can manage,' she said, mustering her feeble reserves. *Gosh, she was so tired.* She stood up, tugging the long tee down, and headed through the door, closing it behind her and waiting for his voice.

'Don't lock it.'

Right on cue. 'I won't,' she promised wearily.

Not so long ago they'd never bothered to shut the bathroom door, but those days were long gone, and for what? Just a lonely, aching wilderness of wasted emotion.

Her eyes prickled and she screwed her eyes up and swallowed hard. She was *not* going to cry. Not, not, not.

And then her head swam again, and the sob she'd tried to suppress wasn't having any of it, and it broke free in an anguished wail.

He opened the door and found her still sitting there, her hand clamped over her mouth. Holding down the sobs? Pointless, because they were escaping anyway and tearing him apart.

The darkening blue tinge of her bruises was starting to show more clearly against the pale skin of her leg. When they really came out it would be black from top to bottom. He dragged his eyes away and swallowed hard. How she hadn't broken anything…

'What's up, sweetheart?' he asked gently, the endearment slipping out past his guard as he went over to her.

'I feel dizzy and I daren't get up and I feel so stupid—'

Her voice cracked, and his hands cradled her head tenderly against him while he told her she wasn't stupid, just hurt, letting her lean on him in a rare moment of weakness while he struggled to keep his own emotions in check. She didn't give him long, though. A few precious seconds at most, and then she pulled herself together, straightening up and using his hands to lever herself to her feet, her independence fighting fit again.

'Thank you,' she said, aiming for the basin, but he headed her off.

'No. Bed,' he told her firmly, wheeling her out of the room towards it. Independence be damned. 'I'll wash your hands, and then I'm going to find us something proper to eat because I think you're probably feeling lightheaded because of low blood sugar as much as anything else. What do you fancy?'

She sat down on the bed and shrugged. 'I don't think there is much. I'd be fine with more toast.'

'That isn't enough, not for either of us, and I haven't eaten all day apart from that muffin which really doesn't count. Don't worry, I'll find something in the freezer. You just settle back and get comfortable and leave it all to me.'

He went back into the bathroom and noticed a tiny crumpled heap of something on the floor beside the pan. The hideous disposable paper pants the hospital had given her, he realised, and stooped slowly and picked them up. She used to wear gorgeous undies—delicate lace that offered tantalising glimpses of her body.

He dropped them in the bin, turned on the tap, ran it until the water was hot and squeezed out her facecloth in the water, adding a touch of soap.

'Here,' he said, picking up her hands one at a time and washing them meticulously. The right one was fine, the left a little grazed and bruised on the outside edge where she must have landed on it, and he worked carefully round the sore place, then rinsed the cloth and wiped them again before patting them dry. Such a simple thing to do, and yet strangely symbolic. If only he could wash away their sadness and make them whole again...

'Thank you,' she whispered, and he looked

up and saw the sparkle of tears in her eyes and felt his own fill. 'Thank you for looking after me. I know I've been horribly ungracious, but I really couldn't have managed without you, and I'm sorry.'

'Oh, Liv—' His voice cracked, and he squeezed her hands in his. 'You don't have to apologise to me for anything.'

'Yes, I do, for so many things—'

'No. Not now. Now, you need to rest, and you need some food, and then you need to sleep,' he said gently, his voice sounding like sandpaper.

He took the towel back into the bathroom and caught sight of his face in the mirror. He looked haggard, his eyes a little wild, his mouth a grim line. No wonder. She could have died under those wheels, so easily. Another foot—

He hung up the towel, rinsed the facecloth and wrung it out so hard he nearly tore it in two.

Nick went downstairs to make some food, and she rested her head back and closed her eyes. She was exhausted, but even on the normally very comfortable bed she couldn't get truly comfortable. She must have dozed off, though, because she woke with a little groan to find he was there again, straddling the small bedroom chair he'd turned around, arms folded across the back, watching her with those intent, searching eyes.

'Hi,' he said, his voice sounding a little rough and unused for some reason.

'Hi. I didn't hear you come back up. Have I been asleep for long?'

'Ten minutes, perhaps?'

'Oh. Right. Not long, then. Did you find any food?'

His mouth kicked up in a wry smile and he shook his head. 'Not really. I had a look in the freezer, but it's not exactly over-stocked. How about a takeaway?'

Her stomach rumbled, and she realised she was ravenous. No wonder she was dizzy. 'That would be lovely.'

'Is the Chinese restaurant on the front still open?'

'Yes. And they deliver free.'

'Special chow mein?' he asked.

Gosh. Had she really been so predictable? It felt odd, especially considering she hadn't had one for at least a year, or maybe two. Not since long before he'd left. She dredged up a smile. 'Please.'

'Banana fritters?'

'That's disgusting,' she said, trying not to be tempted.

'But you love them.'

'Loved,' she corrected. 'I'm eating much more healthily now.'

'Still having chow mein.'

'Says the man whose entire diet today has been a slice of toast, a chocolate muffin and black coffee—and this whole takeaway thing was your idea, remember, not mine.'

His mouth twitched, but he let it go and pulled out his phone, looking for the number.

'Seven six four, three two nine,' she said, and he laughed as he keyed it in, the sound wrapping round her and cloaking her in grief for all they'd lost.

'You always did have the memory of an elephant for irrelevant detail,' he teased, and she felt her smile falter.

'It's not just the irrelevant things I can remember,' she told him sadly, and he swallowed hard and looked away.

'Frankly, today, I'm happy that you can remember anything—yeah, hi, can I order a special chow mein and chicken chop suey with boiled rice, please?'

That made her blink. Normally he'd have had king prawn balls in batter with special fried rice, and drenched the lot in lurid orange sweet and sour sauce, but maybe she wasn't the only one to address her diet. She ran her eyes over him, reassessing the changes she'd noticed earlier. He'd lost a little weight, but it was more than that—the difference between healthy and letting yourself go. He looked fit and toned again, as if he'd taken up running or rejoined a gym. Gone was the man she'd been married to when it had all fallen apart.

Taking care of himself at last? He must be, and about time. He hung up and turned back to her.

'It'll be here in ten minutes.'

'Great. Thanks. Can you help me sort out the pillows? I can't sit up straight enough to eat and my neck's just not comfortable like this.'

'Sure.'

He sat her up, rearranged the pillows and settled her back against them as if she was made of fragile china.

'Better?' he asked, and she nodded.

'Yes, much. Thank you.' She rested her head back and frowned. 'I feel so guilty. Ben and Daisy were expecting you and she will have cooked, you know what she's like.'

'I know, but it can't be helped and Ben knows I'm staying here and why, and it's just until you're all right.'

'I am all right, Nick. I'm fine—'

His quiet snort of disbelief cut her off. 'Really? So fine you can't get off the loo without help? So fine you can't even move in your sleep without waking up because of the pain?'

He came over to her, perched carefully on the edge of the bed and wrapped her hand in both of his, a frown furrowing his brow.

'Liv, look at yourself,' he said softly, his voice oddly raw. 'You're going to be black and blue, your head's banging like a drum—how bad do you have to be before you'll let go of this ridiculous pretence that you're fine and just accept my help? For God's sake, you could have died—'

His voice cracked, his fingers tightening on

hers, and in the moments before he looked away, she saw the fear that he must have felt for her, the guilt that because he'd followed her when she was trying to get away, she'd stepped out in front of the car. And he'd only wanted to talk to her. How much would it have hurt her to stop and listen, give him a chance? Not this much.

'Nick, I didn't look where I was going. It's my fault, not yours.'

He let go of her hand and stood up, pacing to the window.

'Of course it's my fault. It's all my fault. It's my fault our marriage went wrong, it's my fault you threw me out, my fault you got hit—'

'That's rubbish. And it's not your fault our marriage went wrong; I shut you out, I wouldn't let you help me, and if I'd gone to the conference with you instead of sending you on your own, none of this would have happened and I wouldn't have kicked you out. You can't take the blame for everything, Nick. I was horrible to you.'

He sat back down on the bed, taking her hand again, his warmth curiously comforting.

'No, you weren't. You were just unhappy, and so was I, and we took it out on each other instead of getting help, and it just got into a downward spiral and I don't think we knew how to stop it. And it happens so often with couples who have difficulty conceiving, but one thing my job's taught me is that struggling on alone isn't the answer and we were barely even communicating by the end. We got so lost that we couldn't find a way out and we just stopped talking to each other.'

'Why us?' she asked forlornly, but he just shrugged.

'Why anyone? It's the luck of the draw, Liv, and we got unlucky, but it was our own fault we let it destroy us and we both should have known better and tried harder instead of building walls around ourselves.'

The doorbell rang, and he let go of her hand and went downstairs, and she dropped her head back against the pillows.

Was that what they'd done? Built walls? Probably. They'd had an amazing marriage, filled with love and laughter and tenderness, and then bit by bit it had all slowly disappeared, eaten away by the bitter disappointment of their repeated failure to make a baby. And with every bit that went, they'd added another brick to their walls.

Nick was right. It was nobody's fault, and they'd been helpless to help themselves, and by the end they weren't even trying to, they'd just let it all wither away to dust.

A tear trickled out of the corner of her eye, and she swiped it hastily away as he came back into the room with two bowls and a couple of forks.

He plonked himself down on the bed next to her, propped himself up against the headboard and handed her the chow mein. 'There you go, wrap yourself around that.'

It smelt amazing, and there'd be plenty of time to talk later. 'Gosh, I'm ready for this,' she said, finding a smile from somewhere, and dug her fork in.

'Where are you going to sleep?'

He glanced at her, looked around the room and shrugged. 'On the floor, I guess.'

'Nick, there are two other bedrooms—'

'Three.'

She looked away. 'Two. I turned the little room into a study.'

The room that had been destined to be a nursery. The room that had haunted her until she'd had the guts to address it and claim it as her own, instead of waiting for something that would never happen.

He frowned slightly. 'There's a study downstairs.'

'But that's yours,' she said simply, 'and I wanted my own space.' One where she wasn't constantly bombarded by reminders of him. 'I'm doing a course on natural childbirth and pain relief in labour. I'm studying hypnosis at the moment. And it wasn't as if it was needed for anything else.'

He closed his eyes briefly, and when he opened them she could see the anguish in them.

'I'm sorry, Liv,' he said heavily. 'I'm so sorry it didn't work for us, that we never needed that room. I'm sorry I couldn't give you a baby. And I'm so sorry I wasn't there for you, sorry I shut you out, sorry I let you shut me out. It wasn't meant to be like that. Not at all. It was all going to be perfect—'

'Oh, Nick, don't—' She felt her eyes fill and looked away, blinking hard. They'd been so happy, had so many hopes and dreams, and it had all come to nothing and in such a horrible way.

'So anyway,' she went on, putting that firmly out of her mind, 'you have two other rooms to choose from tonight, both of them better than sleeping on the floor.'

'Not for keeping an eye on you, which is after all why I'm here.'

'It's not as if you'll be far away, and anyway, I'm—'

'If you tell me once more that you're fine, I might just strangle you. And I'm not leaving you alone, Liv. Not for anything. I told Sam I'd look after you because otherwise he wouldn't have let you come home, so humour me, for God's sake.'

She gave a choked little laugh. Anyone less physically violent than Nick she'd never met, and he was obviously worried sick about her and she knew he'd only lie awake all night.

'Oh, for goodness' sake, if you're going to insist on being in here, why don't you just sleep in the bed?' she said softly.

After a pause so long she thought he hadn't heard, he turned his head and met her eyes.

'You'd let me do that?'

She frowned. 'Why not? It's not like I can't trust you. You wouldn't be here if I didn't trust you. I would have stayed in hospital.'

'That's not what I meant. I just thought you wouldn't want me that close. It's not much more than an hour since you insisted you needed nightclothes on, and that's when you thought I'd be in another room.'

'That's nothing to do with this.'

'Isn't it?'

'No. It's because I didn't want to—' She didn't know how to describe it. Flaunt herself? In front of Nick? Ridiculous. He knew every inch of her. Expose herself to humiliation, then, perhaps, because he'd certainly lost interest in her body by the end...

He let out a weary sigh. 'Liv, it's OK. I'm sorry, I don't want to argue. Of course you want to wear a nightdress, you're entitled to your privacy. And it doesn't matter where I sleep. I'll sleep anywhere.'

'So sleep here,' she said, patting the mattress beside her. 'Near to me. Just in case—you know...'

He frowned. 'Is your headache worse?'

She tried to shake it, and thought better of it. 'No. No more than it was, and maybe less, but I know you'll be getting up and down all night because you'll be worried about me. If you're here you can just prod me and ask if I'm all right and go straight back to sleep.'

Fat chance.

He hovered over her while she washed, then did a quick neuro check before he settled her in bed and lay down beside her, but he was reluctant to move in case he hurt her or disturbed her, and his head was too full of the endless re-run of the accident to let him sleep.

Beside him Liv was restless and he wasn't sure she was asleep, either, despite the fact that she must be exhausted. Too sore? Or too cold?

The heating must have gone off and the room was growing steadily colder. It hadn't been overwarm in the first place—to save money? He propped himself up on one elbow and peered at her in the dim light spilling in from the landing, and realised she'd kicked the covers off, and she was going to be stiff and sore enough when she woke in the morning.

He checked his phone for the time. Nearly one o'clock. Time for another check. He turned towards her, pulling the covers back over her as he woke her.

'Liv?'

'Mmm?'

'Talk to me, sweetheart. It's time for another check. Are you OK?'

'I'm fine,' she said. She sounded tired rather than sleepy, and he wondered if she'd been awake, too.

'Do you hurt?'

'No, not so much now. I'm a bit cold.'

'You'd kicked the covers off, but I've put them back now, you'll soon warm up.'

He'd propped himself up on one elbow to flash the pen light in her eyes, and it gave him a chance to study her face. The bruise around her eye had invaded the lower lid now, and he could see further bruising along her cheekbone.

Without thinking, he leant over and touched his lips lightly to the bruise. 'You've got a real shiner now,' he said softly. 'The neighbours are going to think I've come back for revenge and beaten you up.'

'You'd never hurt me,' she said quietly. 'Not physically, at least.'

No. She was right, he wouldn't. Couldn't. But it hadn't stopped him walking out on their broken marriage and he knew how badly that had hurt her. Hurt both of them. He sighed softly, lifting his hand and trailing it lightly over her cheekbone and down her jaw. 'Do you need painkillers again?'

'No, not really.' She hesitated, her gaze holding his, then said quietly, as if she was afraid of his reaction, 'Do you know what I really want more than anything? A hug. I've really missed your hugs.'

A tear slid out of the corner of her eye and ran down into her hair, and his eyes blurred.

'Oh, Liv—'

His voice hitched, and he put the pen light back and lay down, reaching out his arms and folding them gently round her, and as she wriggled closer he pressed his lips to her forehead and squeezed his eyes tight shut to try and hold back the tears.

She wasn't the only one who'd missed this, and the feel of her body against his made something deep within him, something that had been out of kilter for one or maybe even two years, fall back into place.

He felt her hand slide up his chest and settle against his jaw, her fingertips resting against his neck, right over the pulse.

'What happened to us, Nick?' she asked sadly, her fingertips stroking soothingly over the beating artery. 'How did we end up in this mess?'

He swallowed hard. 'I have no idea. I just know I miss you every single day.'

'I miss you, too. You were my best friend.'

'Don't—'

His arms tightened round her, cradling her against his heart, and he blinked away the stinging tears and pressed another kiss to her hair.

It was stiff and smelt of blood and antiseptic, and he thought of how close she'd come to death, lying there almost under the wheels of that big, heavy car, and the tears squeezed past his lids and trickled across his temple and onto the pillow by her head.

'I nearly lost you today, Liv,' he whispered into the darkness. 'That car was so close—'

Her arms tightened round him, her lips finding his cheek and feathering soft kisses over the damp skin. 'Oh, Nick. I'm sorry I scared you. I was scared, too. I thought I was going to die—'

Her voice cracked, and he cradled her head tenderly against his shoulder. 'Don't be scared any more. You're not going to die, sweetheart, you're going to be fine,' he murmured gently, 'but you need to rest, my love. Just go to sleep. You're safe now. I've got you.'

She made a sleepy, contented noise and settled against him, and he felt the tension going out of her limbs, her breathing growing slow and deep and regular as she drifted off to sleep, but he didn't sleep for a long, long time.

He just held her, feeling the slow rise and fall of her chest with every breath, the warmth of her body against his, and wondered where on earth they went from here.

CHAPTER FIVE

HE WOKE TO the soft, yielding warmth of Liv's body draped over his.

He'd checked her a couple more times in the night and the last time she'd rolled away, but at some point she must have rolled back. He hadn't woken, but his arm was round her and her head was on his shoulder and it felt so familiar, so *right...*

Her arm lay loosely over his chest, her knee wedged down between his thighs, and her body was so close to his he could feel her heart beat.

Which would have been fine, except his body was apparently very happy to have her pressed up tight against it and he wasn't sure they were quite ready for that yet. At least he'd kept his underwear on. It gave him a little privacy, but not nearly enough, and it wasn't going to get any better unless he could somehow ease his leg out from under hers and move away.

He could always wait, he thought. She'd wake up at some point and then he could get his arm out from under her head and unravel the potentially embarrassing tangle of limbs.

But she didn't wake, and she was overdue for another check. He touched her cheek.

'Liv, wake up.'

She made a funny little noise and snuggled closer, her right arm curving down over his ribs, her fingers tucking under his side.

He closed his eyes, swore softly and took her wrist in his hand and eased it back again. 'Liv! Liv, wake up. I have to check you again.'

But she didn't move, just moaned slightly, and his heart went into overdrive. Why couldn't he wake her? Did she have a brain injury after all, and he'd slept through it and missed the signs?

'Liv! Come on. Wake up. Now!'

He shook her arm roughly and her eyes flickered open, blinking in the daylight that seeped in around the curtained windows. She made a soft noise and shifted her head back so she could get him into focus. 'Don't shout at me. What's the matter?'

Relief flooded him and he closed his eyes and

sucked in a breath. 'Sorry. I'm sorry. I couldn't wake you, and I thought...' He couldn't say it, couldn't voice his fears out loud, but he didn't need to.

She blinked again, as if she'd just worked out where she was and what had happened, and she let out her breath on a little sigh and settled back against him. 'Oh, Nick, I'm fine,' she said softly, her hand coming to rest over his heart. 'A bit sore, but my head's much better now. I was just really heavily asleep.'

He felt himself relax, but not much, because their legs were still wrapped together and he really, really needed to get away before she realised quite how much his body was lapping it up.

'Good. I'm glad you're feeling better, but I need to get up. My arm's gone dead and I need to phone the hospital about Judy Richards.'

'Oh. Sorry, you should have said.'

He gave a soft, frustrated laugh. 'I just did. That's why I was trying to wake you.'

'Oh. Right. OK.'

She put her hand on his chest and shifted her

leg, and as she moved it she brushed against him and her eyes widened and she froze.

'Nick?' His name was a soft out-breath, teasing against his skin, and her hand curved against his cheek, the delicate touch unbearably erotic.

Damn. He closed his eyes. 'Sorry. Ignore it, it's just a normal, physiological response,' he muttered, his voice gruff. 'It doesn't mean anything—'

Her lips brushed his. 'Oh. And there I thought you were pleased to see me,' she murmured, a hint of mischief in her voice, but it was a touch husky and he knew if he didn't get out of there soon he was going to lose the plot.

'Very funny,' he said, but she just laughed softly and curled her hand around the back of his head, easing him closer. Her lips met his again, the touch so sweet, so familiar, so agonisingly dear that he let out a soft groan and kissed her back.

Not for long. Just long enough that he knew if he didn't get out of there fast this was going to get well out of control and it was every kind of a bad idea.

He dragged his mouth away from temptation.

'Liv, no,' he said, his voice as firm as he could make it. 'I have to get up.'

'I thought you were,' she said mischievously, but before he could react she laughed again and rolled away.

'Better?'

'Yes, thank you.'

Liar. It was much worse, because he wanted her right back where she'd been, and it wasn't going to happen. He retrieved his arm and groaned.

'What?'

'Just my arm dropping off.'

'So long as that's all...'

He gave a despairing chuckle, swung his legs over the side of the bed and stood up with his back firmly towards her. He hadn't seen Liv in this teasing, mischievous mood for years, and the urge to get back into bed and haul her into his arms was killing him.

'I'll go and phone the hospital and I'll get you some tea while I'm at it.' He grabbed his shirt and headed for the door, shaking his right arm to get the circulation going. 'Ah, dammit,' he muttered again as the blood started to flow back into it.

'Wimp,' she called after him, and he paused on the top step, shoving his arms into the shirt.

'Me, a wimp? You should listen to yourself. The fuss you've been making, anybody would think you'd been hit by a car.'

The sound of her laughter followed him down the stairs to the kitchen, and he couldn't help but smile. She sounded so much better and the relief he felt was profound. For a moment there, when he hadn't been able to wake her—

He cut that thought off before it dragged him back in, phoned the hospital about Judy while the kettle boiled and took her tea up to her, his body now back under control.

She was in the bathroom when he got there and he put the mug down on the bedside table as she opened the door and came out.

'Are you OK?'

'I'm fine, considering I was *hit by a car*. Much less sore than I deserve to be,' she said with a wry grin.

'Good. And you don't deser—'

She reached out and pressed a finger to his

lips, stopping the words. The grin softened to a smile, and he felt his heart thud against his ribs as she dropped her arm and took another step towards him. She was close enough now that he could smell the toothpaste on her breath and feel the warmth radiating off her skin, and she put her arms around him and rested her head on his chest and hugged him.

'Thank you for looking after me last night,' she murmured, and he wrapped his arms around her and dropped a gentle kiss on her matted, bloodstained hair, every cell in his body aware of the soft press of her breasts against his chest, the warmth of her body luring him, reeling him in. Such a bad idea, but his body thought it was great. He dropped his arms.

'You're welcome,' he said gruffly. 'I've put the tea on your bedside table. I'm going to get my stuff out of the car. I could do with a shower and shave.'

She lifted her hand and rubbed the palm over his jaw against the lie of the hair; he heard the stubble rasp against her skin, saw her pupils darken, felt his body react. 'Shame. I rather like you with the morning-after look,' she said with that slightly wicked smile he'd missed so much for so long now.

Her hand was just there, her thumb against his lips. He could turn his head and press his lips to her palm, ease her back into his arms—or he could just step back out of reach and keep what was left of his sanity.

'Liv, don't do this, please. It's hard enough as it is.'

'Mmm. I noticed.'

He groaned and took a step back out of reach, his control at breaking point. 'It's not funny, Liv,' he said gruffly. 'It's so not a good idea. You're hurt, and it's not what I'm here for.'

Her eyes widened and she blinked, her hand falling slowly to her side.

'No. No, I'm sorry. I wasn't—I didn't mean—'

She couldn't finish the sentence, maybe because like him she didn't know quite what to say, what the protocol was in this really rather awkward situation.

'It's OK. It's just—I don't really think...'

Now it was him who couldn't finish, so he gave up on the conversation, pulled on his trousers, ran downstairs and let himself out of the front door, kicking himself every step of the way.

She watched him go, beating what could only be called a hasty retreat, and bit her lip.

He'd seemed so uncomfortable with her touch, as if she'd crossed an invisible line that had somehow appeared between them since they'd got out of bed. Or maybe it had been there all night, and she'd crossed it then too without realising.

She'd certainly been close enough to him when he'd woken her, close enough to feel his reaction. It wasn't unusual, just a spontaneous physiological response, as he'd said, and in the good old days, before the bad ones, they would have taken advantage of it. But today he couldn't get away fast enough, and he'd seemed embarrassed.

And all she'd done was tease him, when actually she'd wanted him to wrap her in his arms again and make love to her like he used to.

She hadn't even thought about it when she'd suggested he share the bed, and although he'd protested, he hadn't refused, and he'd willingly held her most of the night. He'd obviously only done it out of concern because of her head injury, though, and then she'd gone and wrapped herself all round him, and then hugged him and touched him in a way she no longer had any right to touch him.

And maybe he'd moved on. Maybe there was another woman in his life now, a woman who had those rights?

She felt a wave of humiliation, then a hollow ache inside, and without permission her eyes filled with tears. She hadn't even thought about it, but maybe he'd found someone to love, someone who could give him babies, or just someone to have fun with, as they'd had fun in the early days, before it all became about ovulation tests and body temperature fluctuation and counting days on the calendar?

Not that it was any of her business now, since she'd kicked him out without giving him a second chance.

'Oh, Nick...'

She shifted the pillows into a pile and crawled back onto the bed, leaning back against the pillows and kicking herself for reading too much into his kindness last night. Because that was all it had been, of course. Just kindness.

But he said he'd missed her every single day. Was that kindness talking? It hadn't felt like it, and she was sure there had been tears on his cheeks at one point. That didn't seem like simple kindness, and the way he'd held her, as if she was the most precious thing in the world...

She could hear his voice outside through the bathroom window, and wondered who he was talking to at this time of the morning. Bert, probably. Oh, lord. That would open a whole new can of worms.

It was her own fault. She should have stayed in hospital like Sam had wanted her to instead of making such a fuss—or better still, asked Ben not to contact Nick, and then none of this would have happened.

But then she wouldn't have seen him again, and somehow that felt immeasurably worse...

'Morning, Nick.'

Damn. He looked up and saw their old neighbour clipping their rose hedge. Liv's rose hedge, he corrected himself. He supposed he should be grateful Bert was looking after her, but instead he felt resentful and distinctly underdressed.

'Morning,' he grunted, unlocking the car and opening the door, wincing as he stepped back onto a sharp stone in his bare feet.

Bert's voice followed his head into the car. 'I see you're back, then. Hope you don't mind, I'm just tidying up a few bits and pieces I missed. First clip of the season, so she gets the best flowers.'

He ducked his head back out as Bert took a step towards him, shears in hand. 'Back for good, are you?'

He gave a mental sigh and put the old man straight.

'No. Liv had an accident yesterday. I'm just looking after her for a day or two.'

Bert lowered the shears, settling in no doubt for a nice long chat and a few juicy details. 'Oh, I'm sorry to hear that. I hope she'll be all right. Car, was it?'

'No.' Well, it wasn't. Not hers. 'She fell,' he said, which was being massively frugal with the truth, but it was none of Bert's business. 'She's just got a few bruises and scrapes.'

'Oh, dear. Poor Liv. I'll tell Gwen, she'll pop round—'

'No, Bert, really, it's fine. She just needs to rest.'

'Oh, well. Give her our best, then. And you'd better get back inside before you catch your death with those bare feet.'

'Yes, indeed.'

He lifted his overnight bag out of the car, locked it and headed back inside, hearing the irritating click-click-click of the shears as Bert went back to work on the immaculate hedge. He ran upstairs, pausing at the bedroom door.

'I'm going to have a shower, if that's OK?'

'Of course. Was that Bert?'

'Yes. He'd obviously spotted the car and he wanted to know if I was back. I told him you'd fallen and got a few bruises. He was threatening to send Gwen round, probably to interrogate you. God knows what she'd make of your black eye, but I'm sure I'd be implicated. I told him you needed to rest.'

Liv rolled her eyes. 'Good. Thank you. They mean well, but—Gwen kept asking questions when you went, saying things like, "It's such a shame he's gone, we were so looking forward to the patter of tiny feet,' and I just didn't know what to say to her.'

'Tell her to mind her own business,' he said roughly, the mention of those elusive babies catching him on the raw. 'He's cutting the hedge again, by the way, though why he needs to do it before eight o'clock on a Saturday morning defeats me. It doesn't look as if it needs it anyway.'

'It doesn't. He only did it last week but he was saying he'd missed a bit. I couldn't see it. I've told him not to bother, I can do it myself and anyway, I quite like it when it gets a bit wild, but he insists I won't get the best flowers unless it's done early, and I just can't be that churlish.'

Nick snorted, hefting the bag in his hand. 'I'm damn sure I could. I'm going to shower and get dressed, and then I'd better give Sam an update and phone Ben.'

He scooped up his shoes and socks and took everything to the other bathroom, grabbing a towel on the way and locking the door firmly behind him. Not that she was likely to follow him in, but he just needed some guaranteed privacy while he got his thoughts into order because frankly, between watching her almost get killed and then having her plastered over him all night, his head was a mess and his body wasn't much better.

And her touching him like that, hugging him, kissing him, running her hand over his stubble and looking at him with those melting eyes that threatened to lure him in again—

He stared at the shower controls, contemplated cold and decided against it. He'd never been a masochist, and the last twenty-four hours had been tough enough. He turned on the hot, tested the temperature and stepped into the cubicle under the wall of steaming water.

It pounded down on him, and he dropped his head forwards and felt the tension drain away, but it was replaced by relief that she was still alive, and anguish that she'd been hurt at all, by the deep sorrow left in the wake of their break-up and the grief he still felt that he'd never been able to give her the child she so desperately wanted. Might never be able to.

She'd asked what had happened to them, and the answer was nothing. No pregnancy, no baby, no family.

That, rather than Suzanne, was why their marriage had fallen apart. The business with Suze had just been the trigger, the last straw, and if he was honest, he hadn't cared at that point, because he'd been at the end of his tether with their broken relationship.

By asking for a divorce she'd handed him a perfect way out, or so he'd thought, but then she'd never done it, never started divorce proceedings, just left him in limbo waiting for the other shoe to drop. He'd thought she'd be better off without him, but he hadn't been better off without her, and walking out of her life had left a wound that time didn't seem about to heal.

And getting too close to her again too soon could be a disaster, so no more snuggling up in the night, no more hugs, no more tender touches breaking through his defences and laying him wide open to hurt again.

And what about the job? How were they going to cope with working together every day when they were obviously still so attracted to each other? Could he manage to keep his distance?

Did he really want to? Or was he just being

a coward, afraid to try again? Frankly, he had no idea.

He reached for the soap, scrubbed away the memory of her body against his, towelled himself roughly dry—and discovered he'd forgotten to pack his razor.

Damn.

He ran his hand over his beard, hearing the rasp of it against his skin, feeling the touch of her hand against it earlier, and swore softly and comprehensively at himself.

He could always borrow hers, he supposed, but she'd be unlikely to have a new one and the one in the shower would be worse than useless, he knew that of old. And the intimacy of it…

He'd go and buy some later. Just so she didn't get any more ideas about his morning-after look.

He dressed quickly, packed up his things and took his bag down to the hall. There wasn't really any need to stay here again tonight, he could quite easily go to Ben and Daisy's as planned. Much safer.

He ran back up and stuck his head round the bedroom door. 'OK?'

'Yes, except I'd love more tea. Oh, and Sam

rang, by the way. He's on his way over to check up on me. Says he doesn't trust you.'

'Damn cheek. Do you have any decent coffee?'

'I think so, in the freezer. If not there's an unopened packet of ground coffee in the larder cupboard. I might not have a lot of milk. I was going shopping on the way home.'

'I'll check. What do you want for breakfast?'

She shrugged. 'Anything. Toast is easy. And marmalade. It's in the fridge door. And forget the tea, I'll have coffee if you're making it for Sam.'

'OK.'

He ran downstairs and put the kettle on just as the doorbell rang, and he opened the door to his old friend.

'Sam—come in. Thank you so much for yesterday.'

'You're welcome,' Sam said, stepping into the hall and wrapping Nick in a fierce and affectionate hug. Yesterday he'd been a professional but today he was a concerned friend, and he dropped his arms and stepped back with a wry smile, studying his face.

'It's really good to see you again. I'm just sorry

it was under those circumstances. How is she? And come to that, how are you? It must have been pretty tough to witness it.'

He shrugged and closed the front door. 'I'm fine. She's a bit sore, but her head seems OK and that was the real worry. I've just put the kettle on. Can I get you anything?'

'Coffee would be good. I've been up since before six with Isadora.'

'Your baby?'

'Yes. She was born last October.' Sam smiled ruefully. 'She's gorgeous, but she's an early riser, and Kate's not a morning person.'

'Are you?'

Sam laughed. 'After years in the army, believe me, getting up for a smiley baby is a walk in the park.'

Nick gave a dutiful laugh, then turned away. 'Yes, I can imagine,' he said. 'Why don't you go on up and see Liv? She's on the right at the top of the stairs. I'm just getting her breakfast and I'll bring our coffee up.'

He headed back to the kitchen, trying hard not to think of the joy of being woken by a baby with a beaming smile at any time of the day or night.

Liv hadn't wanted to go to the conference because everyone would be talking about their children, and she'd been right. They were at the age where their friends nearly all had families, and the fact that they'd kept their problems a secret just meant there'd been nobody to share it with, no one to offload on when it all became too much.

Except Suze, and look where that had got him.

He put bread in the toaster, checked the milk situation and found the new packet of coffee and the cafetière.

Core business, he told himself. *Stick to what you're here for, and forget the rest.*

'Well, good morning. How's the patient?'

'Much better but cross with myself, thank you,' she told him, and then asked the question that had been niggling at her since yesterday. 'How come you know Nick?'

'We grew up together. He was my best friend, but we drifted apart once life got in the way.'

'Ah. You're that Sam—the one who taught him to sail,' she said, all the little pieces falling neatly into place.

'That's me. Can we talk about you, now?' he said, smiling a little wryly. 'That's a cracking black eye you've got there.'

'Isn't it just? At least it's only the colour. I can still open my eye more or less fully, and I feel fine now.'

'Really? The eye doesn't say so, and I'm pretty sure your body's at least as colourful.'

'I'm fine, Sam. Really. Yes, I hurt a bit here and there, but I'm alive, no fractures, I haven't got a serious head injury—what more could I ask for? Apart from the common sense not to have stepped backwards off the pavement. That would have helped.'

Sam chuckled, then his smile faded as he studied her. 'How is Nick? I haven't seen him for years. The last I knew he was working in Surrey.'

'He was, but that's six or seven years ago. It's where we met.' She swallowed and looked away. 'And I don't really know how he is. I haven't seen him since last March, and I hadn't spoken to him then since we split up in the middle of January because we weren't working together and we were avoiding each other. He came back yesterday because he's going to locum for a bit, but that was the first time we'd spoken, so yesterday was a bit of a trial, one way or another.'

Sam looked shocked. 'Gosh, Liv, I'm sorry. If I'd realised that, I wouldn't have suggested he stayed here with you, but you seemed to want him around and he certainly wasn't going anywhere, but no wonder you both objected. Ben mentioned that you weren't together now, but I just assumed you had a working relationship—kids, probably, and shared custody, not total radio silence.'

She tried to smile, but it was probably a sad little event and she gave up. 'No kids,' she said, trying to keep the wobble out of her voice. 'We just—it wasn't working, so we split up.'

She didn't elaborate, just left him to conclude whatever he liked from that, because by the end nothing had been working for them, not the relentless striving for a child, or their crumbling relationship.

'I'm sorry,' Sam said again. 'I shouldn't have interfered without knowing more about your situation.'

'Sam, it's fine,' she said, swiftly changing the subject to one she was more comfortable with than the slow and painful disintegration of her marriage. 'Tell me about your baby.'

'Isadora?'

'Is that what you called her? What a lovely name. Have you got any photos?'

Of course he did, and he pulled out his phone and scrolled around for a moment and then handed it to her. 'Swipe from right to left. That's her yesterday morning, helping me eat my breakfast. She kept stealing the spoon, so I think we're going to have to start weaning her soon.'

'She's just like you.'

'I generally have better table manners.'

Liv felt a lump in her throat, and with a choked little laugh she scrolled through the photos, only handing the phone back when Nick came in with a tray laden with toast and coffee.

'Room service,' he said lightly, putting the tray down on the top of her chest of drawers and turning to Sam. 'Black, white, sugar?'

But her head was aching, and she knew the men would have lots to talk about, so she caught Nick's eye. 'Actually, I could do with a nap. If you could leave me some toast and coffee, maybe you two would like to catch up downstairs for a while?'

* * *

Sam stayed for an hour, telling him about the baby, his wife, their house, the fact that he'd just bought, done up and sold a wooden ketch and was now looking for a much more sensibly sized sailing dinghy.

'I thought I might get a Laser or a Firefly. You'll have to come out with me when I get it. I'd trust you not to tip us both over the side,' he said with a wry grin, and Nick laughed, remembering the time Sam had taken a girl out sailing and she'd done exactly that.

'I can still hear that girl scream as she hit the water,' he said with a chuckle, and Sam grinned.

'Lizzie. Yeah. She never really forgave me for that.'

His smile died, and he searched Nick's face with eyes that knew him far too well.

'I'm sorry about you and Liv. She's a lovely woman.'

'She is,' he said, that lump back in his throat, 'but it just wasn't working any more.'

'Yes, she said. Shame.'

'It is, but it's over, we've moved on, and—well,

that's it, really,' he lied, glossing over a whole world of messy emotions.

'So I gather you're going to be locuming here for a bit.'

'Yes.' He looked away, pretending to study his hands. 'I don't know how I feel about it. Coming back here, I mean.'

'How does Liv feel?'

'I don't know. I tried to talk to her about it yesterday but it didn't go well. I didn't realise we'd be working together, I thought she'd be in the midwife-led unit still, so yesterday was a bit fraught, and since I almost killed her by letting her fall under a car, we've had other things to think about.'

Sam put his cup down and got to his feet.

'I'll leave you in peace. It'll be good to have you near for a while, though, and let's not lose touch this time. It's been way, way too long and I didn't realise how much I'd missed you.'

He hugged Nick again, the gesture saying more than words ever could, and Nick waved him off and closed the door. The lump in his throat was so big now he could hardly swallow.

What on earth was wrong with him today? He was an emotional wreck—

'Has Sam gone?'

He turned slowly and looked up the stairs at Liv. She must have showered, because her hair was wet and she was wearing a loose, comfortable dress that fell to her ankles. He was glad about that. It covered her bruises, which meant he wouldn't be constantly reminded of them. If he didn't look at her face...

'Yeah, he's gone. I thought you were napping? Did he say it was OK to wash your hair?'

She nodded. 'He said it would be fine so long as I didn't soak in the bath, so I just showered to get the blood off, really. I feel much better now. Much less sore and a lot less grubby.'

'Good. Will you be OK if I go out? I need to see Judy Richards, and Ben wants to talk to me about the job and what it entails which he was going to do yesterday evening, so I thought I'd walk to the hospital, then I can pick up your car after I'm done.'

'Good thinking. I'll get a parking fine if I don't move it but I'm not sure I should drive yet. You know what insurance companies are like,' she said, making her way carefully down the stairs. 'And you also need to apologise to Ben for me for messing up your weekend—and don't tell me again it was your fault.'

He ignored that. 'I'll pick up some more milk while I'm out. Is there anything else you want?'

She nodded. 'Maybe some salad for lunch and something to have with it? Oh, and probably bread. I don't have any decent bread.'

'OK. Text me a shopping list—and I need the car key.'

'I'll just give you my set. There's a house key on there as well, so you'll be able to let yourself back in, just in case I have a nap on the sofa.'

She found them in her bag and then hesitated before she dropped them into his outstretched hand, as though she was afraid to touch him. Very wise. He closed his fist around them, nodded, and let himself out.

CHAPTER SIX

SHE SPENT THE morning dozing on the sofa in the sitting room.

It was the sofa she'd always thought of as his, the only one she used now. It had the best view of the garden, if you didn't count the one from what they'd optimistically described as the family room, and she hadn't been able to bring herself to sit in there since their final showdown.

Too many painful memories.

But it had been glorious in the sitting room today, the sun streaming in and bringing the promise of spring with it, and between that and her sleepless night she'd struggled to stay awake, but lying awkwardly hadn't done her neck any good so she'd retreated back to the bedroom for a nap.

She was contemplating getting up and taking a walk around the garden when she heard the scrape of the key in the lock and his soft, 'Hello? I'm back,' as he closed the door.

'I'm up here,' she called, and she heard him run lightly up the stairs, tapping on the door as he walked in.

The Nick she'd fallen in love with wouldn't have knocked, and he would have bent down and kissed her, but this Nick didn't, and it was shocking how much she'd missed that. How much she'd missed him.

'I'm sorry I've been so long. Have you been OK?'

'I've been fine. Sleeping, mostly. How's Judy?'

'Good. Everything's stable, the baby's got a lovely strong heartbeat, her blood pressure's fine and the placenta scan was OK. It's just watch and wait until the blood test results come back. I got milk. Do you want a coffee?'

'That would be great. Thanks.'

He disappeared for a little while, and she could hear the kettle boiling and the sound of the fridge door being opened and shut as he put the shopping away, then after a moment he came back up the stairs with the coffee and a packet of almond thins.

'My favourite biscuits!'

He opened the packet and handed them to her, his smile a little crooked. 'We aim to please.'

'How did you get on with Ben?'

'All right,' he said thoughtfully. He put the biscuits down on the bed and propped himself up against the headboard beside her, his face troubled. 'There's a possibility Simon won't come back.'

'I did wonder. Was Ben trying to talk you into staying?'

He chuckled quietly. 'How did you guess? I said I'd do the locum partly to help Ben out of a bind and partly because I knew I needed to see you again, but we haven't exactly got off to a flying start and I wouldn't contemplate coming back permanently if you didn't want me to, Liv. That wouldn't be fair on either of us.'

'No. No, it wouldn't.' She bit her lip, wondering what it would be like if he came back, and she realised she was hoping—desperately hoping—that it would happen. But only if he came back to her as well, and there was a question that was burning a hole in her, even though she wasn't sure she'd want the answer despite agonising over it the whole time he'd been out—well, when she hadn't been asleep, at least—but it was sort of relevant so she said it anyway.

'That would depend on if there's anybody else in your life now, because that would change things a lot. You know—someone you're seeing? Suzanne, perhaps, or someone new?'

His laugh sounded like disbelief, and he shook his head firmly. 'No, Liv. Absolutely not, and certainly not Suze. I haven't even seen her since the conference. I've been working in a different field so our paths don't cross any more, and even if they did, our relationship was over seven years ago. Why would I want to go back to it? And, no, there isn't anyone else, either. There hasn't been anyone else. I'm not interested.'

She stared at him, shocked by that admission. Her relationship with Nick was—or had been—physical. Very physical. Until it all went so horribly wrong.

'No one at all?' she asked incredulously. 'Not even a minor fling, in more than a year?'

He shook his head. 'No. Why would I?'

'For sex?' she offered, stating the obvious, and got the same sad, slightly disbelieving laugh.

'With someone I don't really want? No. Sex is just an itch, Liv. I can scratch it myself, and the only woman I really want threw me out, so that's not a goer.'

He held her eyes with his, the sincerity in them so believable she couldn't doubt it, and after an age she sucked in a breath and looked away, letting it all sink in, but still it didn't quite stack up, because always in the background was this thing with Suzanne that she couldn't quite believe.

'If that's really true, can we scroll back to the conference, because it doesn't seem plausible that you'd be in your room with Suze and not sleep with her, and I'm obviously not the only person who thought that. I knew something had been going on because Beth rang me on Sunday morning and asked if everything was all right, and there was just something in her voice that told me it wasn't, and when she said Suzanne was there and she'd seen you together at breakfast, it all sort of fell into place. But breakfast alone wouldn't make her think that, surely, so she must have seen you going into your room together, and I'm really struggling with that because I know you, Nick, and I know sex is a hugely significant thing in your life, so if it wasn't to sleep with Suze, then what the hell *was* it for?'

He was staring down at his coffee, his face a mask, shutting her out again.

'I just needed to talk to her,' he said eventually.

'So why couldn't you do that downstairs in the bar or something? Why your room? And what on earth were you doing that made Beth suspicious enough to ring me?'

He let out a weary sigh and scrubbed his hand through his hair, then he lifted his head and met her eyes, and his were raw with pain and grief.

'She saw us waiting for the lift. I was in the bar on my own wallowing in self-pity, and Suze came over and asked me if I was all right, and I got so choked I couldn't answer her, so she suggested we took it upstairs. She grabbed the bottle of wine off the table and hauled me out of the bar, and I didn't stop to analyse what anyone might think of it. I just wanted to leave before I made a total idiot of myself, and then we ran into Beth by the lift—me, Suze and the bottle. God knows what she thought we were up to but it must have looked pretty incriminating. Anyway, she asked how we were and I mumbled something and then the lift came and we got in it. Then the following morning she came into the restaurant after we'd already met up there, saw us having breakfast together and I guess put two and two together and came up with five.'

'Well, of course she would—who wouldn't?'

'Exactly. And under any normal circumstances and with anybody else, she would have been right, but it wasn't normal, I wasn't normal, and Suze realised that. That's why she got me out of there, and I can promise you sex was absolutely the last thing on my mind at the time.'

'So why didn't you just tell me that?'

'Because you wouldn't have believed me, and because for that fleeting moment it seemed like an escape route and I was desperate for one. It was a split-second decision, Liv, and I've regretted it ever since, and I know it's too late now to undo all the hurt, but I really need you to believe that nothing happened between me and Suze.'

'So—what did you do? You just drank the bottle of wine and talked? And if so, how did she come to write you that note? "Always here if you need me"? I don't buy it. That's a lover's note, Nick.'

'Or a friend's. If she hadn't been there that night I don't know what would have happened to me, because I was on the brink of a total meltdown and if it hadn't been for her I don't know what I would have done. And I know she's not a saint, but she's not a whore, and that was a cheap shot yesterday, Liv.'

She felt a wash of shame. 'I know. I'm sorry, I should never have said that but I'd spent a year hating her—'

'No. You've spent seven years hating her, being jealous of her, and I've never understood it.'

'What? She's gorgeous, Nick. She's got that amazing lush figure and come-to-bed eyes and you were together for years. And I know she's still in your phone contacts, and she sends you a Christmas card every year—it really wasn't such a stretch to think you would have slept with her again. A lot of people wouldn't even count it, sleeping with an ex.'

'But I would. Which is why I couldn't have done it, because she's a *friend* now—and anyway, what makes you think she's any more desirable than you are?' he asked, shifting so that he was facing her.

'Because I'm not blind?'

He laughed softly and shook his head. 'Liv—seriously, you have nothing to worry about in that department. Yes, we were lovers, of course we were, but she didn't want what I wanted, she didn't see life and family and the future in the same way as me, but you did, and right from the beginning I knew I needed to be with you. You're the one I married, you're the only woman I'll ever want.'

'But you didn't want me then! We hardly ever made love any more, only when the time was right, and it wasn't as if you hadn't slept with her before, so why not?'

'I've just told you that—and I did still want you. I just couldn't touch you without breaking down, and I was trying to be strong for you but I just couldn't do it any longer. I was breaking my heart over us, Liv, and Suze realised it, and the moment the door was shut and she said, "What's wrong?", I fell apart. She sat me on the bed and held me, and I unravelled all over her.

'When I finally ground to a halt she made us

coffee and let me talk. Which I did, for hours. I lay on the bed next to her and poured my heart out, told her everything, and then I fell asleep and when I woke up, she was gone. She must have written the note and put it in my bag before she left, but I didn't see it until you showed it to me.

'She told me over breakfast to come home to you and sort things out, to do what I could to mend our marriage, but I'd hardly got through the door before I had to go into the hospital to deliver Amy Zacharelli's baby, and by the time I got back you'd already spoken to Beth, you'd found the note, and you'd made up your mind. From that point on, I didn't stand a chance.'

Tears welled in her eyes, and she looked down at her hands, the fingers clenched together, trying not to cry for everything they'd lost. Or thrown away.

'I'm so sorry. Sorry I've been mean about her… sorry I didn't trust you. I should have trusted you, but the evidence was so clear, Nick, and I felt like such an idiot. That was why I was so shocked about Suzanne, so angry, because even though I was jealous of her I thought I knew you wouldn't do something like that, not once we were married, and then suddenly it looked as if you'd just run back into her open arms and I wondered if I really knew you at all.'

His hand reached out and cradled her cheek gently. 'Of course you know me. There's not much to know. I'm pretty straightforward. You should have trusted your judgement—and I should have told you the truth there and then.'

'But I didn't make it easy for you, did I? As you said, I'd made up my mind, and I'm so sorry, because it's all my own stupid fault. I should have come with you. It should have been me you broke down with, me you poured your heart out to. If I'd only come with you, maybe you would have done that and then all this business with Suze would never have happened,' she whispered, her voice cracking, but he shifted closer, disentangling her knotted fingers and wrapping them in his warm, strong hands.

'No,' he said gruffly. 'It's not your fault, it's mine. I can't let you take the blame for that. I shouldn't have gone, but I was just at the end of my tether with it all and I couldn't cope with it any more. I'd had the day from hell, and then I came home and found you distraught because you weren't pregnant again and I couldn't take it any more, couldn't bear your pain any more. It was the last straw.

'I never should have left you alone like that. I should have stayed with you, talked about it properly, faced the truth instead of just running away to the conference because it was the easiest thing to do—'

'What could you have done? We'd talked about it endlessly. Every month, for nearly two years. What more was there to say? We'd said it all.'

'No, we hadn't. We'd said the same things over and over. It'll be all right. It'll happen soon, we just need to give it time. We're still young. There's no hurry. Lots of people have this trouble. We've been too busy. We missed the date—every month, the same excuses, the same justification for our failure to conceive, but we never once admitted that we might have a problem, that we needed help, that it wasn't working and wasn't going to work, because we didn't want to admit it. It was as if saying it out loud would make it real, and we couldn't bear to do that.'

She didn't answer, because she didn't need to. He was right, all their talking had got them nowhere because neither of them would admit that they needed help, and maybe there would have been a simple answer if they'd only ever asked the right question.

She'd started running for an hour every day to escape from the truth, from the mess her marriage was in, from the endless recurring sorrow of her infertility, and yet the running itself might have made the situation worse. Why hadn't she realised that? She'd got so thin, scrawny almost. That wasn't healthy, but it hadn't stopped her, and there had been the odd month when the ovulation test hadn't reacted positively. Was that why?

His thumb traced idly over the back of her hand, sweeping backwards and forwards, over and over as the silence hung in the air between them until finally he broke it with a shuddering sigh.

'I wish I'd felt able to talk to you, Liv. I never really told you how I felt, did I? Not really. Not honestly. I never told you how I grieved for us every time we failed, how I ached for you, how

I blamed myself for not being able to help you when I was working in the same field. Why couldn't I? I'm a doctor, an obstetrician. My job is babies, and yet I couldn't even give you a baby.'

'You weren't alone, Nick. My job's babies, too, and I couldn't give you one, either. And I couldn't talk about it—not to you, not to anyone. I don't think that helped us.'

'No, I don't think it did. I meant to, when I got back from the conference, but then the whole thing just escalated and overwhelmed me, and I wasn't thinking clearly anyway. I'd had virtually no sleep, I knew I had a mountain to climb to get our marriage back on track, and then you told me to go and I realised there wasn't any point in talking about it, because you'd made up your mind, so I did the easy thing. Again. It was about the only thing I was any good at.'

'So why not talk to me after that?' she asked. 'You were still here for nearly three months, working your notice. You could have given me time to cool off, and then told me the truth. I waited and waited, and you never said a word in your own defence. It felt like you'd slunk away with your tail between your legs, and it just made you look even guiltier, if that was possible.'

'I know, and it was deliberate, even though it was killing me. I thought it would be easier that way, easier for both of us—give us a fresh start. I thought we might be able to move on, but I haven't. I haven't moved on at all. Have you?' he asked, his voice low, the question hardly voiced as if he wasn't sure he wanted the answer. 'Have you met anyone?'

She shook her head. 'No. No, of course not.'

'There's no "of course" about it. You're a beautiful woman, Liv. Why not?'

Because no one else was Nick. She'd had other relationships before she'd met him, but once he'd come into her life she'd realised he was the only man she'd ever really loved, the only man she'd ever really wanted. Nothing would change that.

She shook her head. 'I'm not interested. I've never been one for casual sex, and even if I'd met someone I really liked, I wouldn't have done anything about it, because the last thing I needed was another relationship. I just can't see it happening.'

'Because I hurt you so badly,' he said heavily.

'No, not you. Our marriage. The way it slowly crumbled away beneath us. That was so hard to take, and it wasn't even as if we'd fallen out of love. We'd just stopped communicating.'

'We had, you're right. And we shouldn't have done, but I was afraid if I was honest and told you how desperate I was, you'd just feel even guiltier, and I knew how that felt.'

She looked up at him, searching his eyes while she asked another question, one which had been plaguing her since Ben had told her what he'd been doing.

'I know I've already asked you this, but why *are* you working in infertility? I would have thought you'd run screaming from it, taken any other job in the world, almost, to avoid it.'

He shrugged and shifted on the bed, and she wriggled closer and rested her head on his shoulder.

'I don't know, to be honest,' he murmured. 'It was partly by accident, really. As soon as he knew it was destined for closure the consultant left to set up his own private clinic, and they were left in the lurch without a proper job to offer, so recruiting someone permanent wasn't possible, and I'd just come to the end of one job, it was in the same department, I knew some of the people—I suppose I felt I owed them, in a way, and they talked me into it. I didn't really want to do it, but it wasn't long term, there was a definite end-date, and I thought it would give me time to look for something I really wanted. And it meant I wouldn't have to move again for a while. So I said yes, and then after a bit I realised I'm actually ideally placed to do it.

'I know what it's like, I know what they go through, how hard it can be to cope with the endless see-saw of emotions, the hope, the fear, the despair, and in a way it helped me to understand what had happened to us. As I told you yesterday, I realised we're definitely not alone. There are marriages and relationships falling apart all the time because of the pressure couples put on themselves, and for the ones who stick together, if I can help them get pregnant, then maybe I can save them going through what we did, and if I can't, I can empathise. I can give them advice, point them in the direction of support groups, talking therapies, relationship advice—'

'We never had any of that,' she pointed out sadly.

'No. No, we didn't. Nor did we go through the endless investigations, or try any one of the many options which might have helped us in one way or another, and I'm still not really sure why, because it was getting blindingly obvious that we needed help. Maybe it was because we felt there wasn't enough there to start with, that our marriage just wasn't strong enough to survive what might lie ahead.'

She sucked her breath in, shocked by that. 'Nick, we had a good marriage,' she said, her voice little more than a whisper. 'You know we did.'

'I thought so. I'd always thought so, so why couldn't I support you when you needed me?' he asked despairingly. 'Why wasn't I there for you every time it didn't happen? Why did I go to the conference without you that weekend— and why did you believe the worst of me and not even question me about Suze?'

'I did!'

'No. You asked me if she was in my room. You never asked me why, or what we did. You just assumed I'd slept with her, and yes, I could have explained, but it was as if you'd already made up your mind, and in the next breath you told me you wanted a divorce as if you'd been waiting for a reason to get rid of me. Why would you do that if our marriage was so good?'

'Because it wasn't by then,' she admitted, her eyes filling. 'It was awful. You know what it was like. We hardly spoke to each other, we never hugged or kissed or laughed together. We just had sex at the right time—never at the wrong time, never just because we wanted to. I can't remember when we last made love, but I can remember just about every time we had sex to make a baby that never happened.'

He was silent for an age, and then he drew in a ragged breath and rested his head against hers.

'I'm sorry. I never meant it to be like that, but this room became such an emotional minefield that I almost dreaded going into it. I felt as if that was all you wanted from me, that I was just a sperm donor, that my only reason for being there was to get you pregnant, and I couldn't do that, and when you said you wanted a divorce, it gave me a way out of a situation that was tearing me apart.'

'Which was why you didn't tell me the truth about that night, because you wanted out.'

'Partly. I knew I still loved you, and I was coming home to try and make it work, but in my heart of hearts I knew I couldn't live with you any more, not the way it was. And I don't want to go there again, Liv, I really don't. I won't get back on that merry-go-round of hope and despair until I'm sure we're strong enough to take the next step. It's too destructive, and I can't do it. It just hurts too damn much.'

'Have I asked you to?'

He shook his head. 'No. No, you haven't, but I didn't want you building any dreams of that happening on the vague possibility of me coming back here to work permanently. That's not what I'm here for, and I don't know if we could ever be strong enough to try again for a baby.'

Her heart jolted, a shock of disappointment coursing through her, and she realised she'd foolishly allowed herself to hope...

'So why did you say yes to Ben? Why did you come back?'

'Because I have to earn a living?'

She waited, but he said nothing more for a long time, then eventually he shrugged his shoulders as if he was asking himself the same question.

'I don't know,' he said at last. 'Yes, I needed to work, but I could have taken any one of a number of locum jobs. I wasn't even going to start looking until I'd had a holiday, but then Ben rang, and—I don't know why I'm here really, Liv. I just know I'm not happy, that my life outside work doesn't really exist, that I'm lonely and I miss our old friends.'

He turned towards her, and she shifted her head so she could look into those sad, stormy eyes.

'And I miss you,' he went on softly. 'All the time. I know I hurt you, and I know you hurt me, but I still miss you, and I never stopped loving you, which doesn't mean I see us getting back together, but maybe we can find something else, forge a friendship—I don't know. I don't have the answers, Liv, I wish I did. I just know that what I have now isn't working for me, either in terms of job satisfaction or personally, and

I want more. I want something better. And one way or another, I want you in my life.'

She held his eyes, her own filling. 'I want you, too. I've missed you every single day. And even though it was horrible by the end, I still loved you. I'll always love you. And I want something better, too, because there has to be something better than this.'

He gave a quiet, heartfelt sigh. 'That's why I came back, but just because we love each other doesn't mean it works, Liv, and we've hurt each other enough already. The last thing I want is to make it any worse.'

She gave a soft huff of empty laughter. 'I don't think that's possible,' she said honestly, and he sucked in a breath, his fingers tightening on hers.

'Don't say that. I didn't want to hurt you. I never wanted to hurt you.'

Their eyes were locked, his sorrow and regret plain to see until in the end he sucked in a shuddering breath and looked away.

'Oh, Nick. Come here,' she said softly, and he shifted, putting his arms around her with such fierce tenderness it made her want to cry. She turned her face into his chest, breathing in the scent that was so unmistakably Nick, holding him close.

'I miss you so much,' she admitted. 'My life's so empty without you. All I have is my work, and I love it, but I'm still empty because you aren't here.'

His arms tightened a fraction, his chest shifting as he sucked in a deep breath, then let it out on a ragged sigh. 'I'm empty, too, but I don't want to go back to what we had.'

'Then let's not. Maybe we should try again, Nick. Not for a baby, but for us, to see if we can make each other happy like we used to. Because we did. We were very happy, once. Maybe we could be happy again, if we wanted it enough. Maybe we just didn't try hard enough at *that*.'

He lifted his head and searched her eyes, then his closed and he swallowed hard.

'I don't know. I don't know if we can even remember *how* to be happy any more.'

'But we should try. We owe ourselves that much.'

She drew his head down, touching her lips to his, and with a quiet sigh he kissed her back, a gentle, lingering kiss, not platonic but not passionate, either.

An apology, from both of them, for all that had gone before?

Then he pulled back a little, staring down into her eyes. 'I'm sorry I blew it,' he said quietly. 'I honestly never meant to hurt you. I thought leaving would make it easier for you, but it didn't, did it? And I don't want to risk hurting you again.'

She sighed quietly, wishing she could see an easy way forward, dreading how she would feel if they couldn't. 'Life hurt us both, Nick, but only because we let it. We're older now, wiser. Why don't we just see where this takes us? You're here for a while now. Maybe we just need to turn back the clock far enough, rediscover what it was about each other that we fell in love with. Maybe that's all we've ever needed. And if we can't have children, we have our jobs and they're filled with babies, all the babies we could ever want. Maybe that should be enough for us. We need to find what it was we had, and then perhaps we'll be able to make sense of it all.'

'Maybe. But I'm not making any promises. Not yet. And I don't want to rush into anything, either. As you said, I'm here for a while. Let's just take our time.'

He dropped another kiss on her lips before rolling away from her and standing up—to distance himself from a conversation that was becoming uncomfortably deep? Probably, because he changed the subject then, his voice firmer, deceptively casual.

'By the way, did you know Daisy's pregnant again?'

'Yes. I'm really pleased for her. She had a miscarriage a few months back, and they were gutted. It's really good news.'

'Ben didn't tell me that,' he said quietly, his attempt at casual banished in an instant. 'That's really sad. Miscarriage is horrible.'

'It's obstetrics, Nick. It happens. Pregnancy is never a certainty until you've got a healthy baby in your arms, and that's just the start of all the trouble. They have to grow up safely, and that can be a challenge. Their little boy Thomas fell out of a tree last year and broke his arm.'

'I didn't know that, either. I can't believe he's old enough to climb trees.'

'No. You disappeared off the radar, Nick, not

just for me but for everybody. It would be so good to have you back, even if it was just as a friend. I've really missed your friendship.'

She reached out a hand and he took it, folding it in both of his, bowing his head to press a firm, lingering kiss on her knuckles.

'Let me think about it, Liv. Don't let's rush this. The last thing I want to do is make any more mistakes.'

She nodded, not wanting to give him time but knowing she had no choice if she was going to stand a chance to win him back. And she really, really wanted him back. She knew that now, with bone-deep certainty.

But first, it was time for a change of scenery, a breath of air, a bit of emotional space for both of them.

'I need to walk around for a bit or I'll just seize up. And I'm starving. How about some lunch?'

CHAPTER SEVEN

SHE WANTED HIM BACK—and he wanted her. That had never changed.

But to try again? He wasn't sure if what he felt was trepidation or anticipation.

Or both. But there were still things she didn't know, things he wasn't sure he wanted to tell her until he knew it was relevant, and the knowledge was eating a hole in him.

He made them lunch, just a simple salad with the things he'd picked up in the local shops on the way back, while she sat in the garden munching almond thins and drinking her tepid coffee on the swing seat under the tree where they'd often sat together in the good old days.

Not so much in the bad old days. She'd tended to retreat to it then, and he'd let her.

A mistake? Probably, but he'd been struggling to stay afloat himself then, and it had all been about self-preservation. He picked up the plates and went out to her.

'Can you manage this on your lap? It's pretty much fork food.'

'That's fine—it looks lovely. Thank you.'

'You're welcome. How are you feeling now?'

'OK. I feel a bit woozy if I bend over, but not bad. I can move around which has to be a good thing. I might go for a stroll later. I don't want to seize up.'

'Don't overdo it.'

She rolled her eyes and went back to her salad, and when she'd finished eating she went into the sitting room to watch the television while he cleared up the kitchen and dealt with his emails.

Mostly spam and trivia, but there was one from Ben with the detailed job description attached, dangling the carrot under his nose again. He read it through carefully, more and more sure that he wanted it if Simon didn't come back— so long as this thing with Liv didn't blow up in both their faces.

He'd do his best to avoid it, but his track record wasn't great. Could they pull it off? He really, really wasn't sure, but the best way to make it work was to take it slowly and give themselves time to adjust, to get used to each other again rather than jumping in the deep end. That way at least they could still be friends, and anything more would just be a bonus.

He stayed there that night, justifying it to himself on the grounds of her head injury—which, considering how well she looked, could have seemed a bogus excuse, but he wasn't prepared to risk it. At the very least she had concussion, and it wasn't too late for a slow, encapsulated bleed to flare into a full-blown crisis, so he talked himself into it and slept in the spare room with the door ajar—just in case.

He woke in the night and went to check on her, and found her fast asleep with her arms wrapped round a pillow.

Better that than him, he thought morosely. A lot, lot safer. Safer still if he found himself a flat. He'd check online tomorrow, see what there was. He went back to bed, ridiculously jealous of the pillow, and finally fell asleep again, to be woken by the brush of her hair over his face and the touch of her lips on his cheek.

'Rise and shine, sleepy-head. I've brought you a cup of tea. I thought you might want it before you go back to the hospital to see Judy Richards again.'

Judy! He struggled up out of the bedclothes, stifling a yawn and the urge to pull her down into the bed with him and take advantage of his early-morning erection. 'What's the time?'

'Eight thirty.'

'Damn. No time for tea. Shoo.' He grabbed the bedclothes, gave her a pointed look and waited until she was out of the room before throwing them off and getting out of bed.

He definitely needed a place of his own.

He showered in record time, went to the hospital and satisfied himself that Judy was all right and her baby was stable, then on the way out his phone rang.

'Nick? It's Sam. What are you up to?'

'I've just seen a patient and I'm leaving the hospital now—why?'

'Because I've been thinking, Ben said you were supposed to be staying with them until you could find a flat, but you didn't sound over-joyed, and after talking to you and Liv yesterday it's pretty obvious you feel awkward staying with her, so why don't you come and live here while you do your locum? We've got a cabin in the garden that's doing nothing and you'll love it—it's right by the sea wall. You probably know it, it used to be James and Connie's house and I lived in the cabin when I first came up here, before I bought the house off them. It's got everything you'd need—a shower room and a small kitchen, a decent bed, free wi-fi, and it would be great for you.'

A place of his own? He felt a wash of relief, but held it down. For now. 'I didn't know you'd bought it—but then I don't know anything about your life now, so that's hardly a surprise, is it? And hadn't you better ask Kate before you start offering me the cabin? She might hate me.'

'Nah, of course she won't. She's itching to meet you, and anyway, it was her idea. Why don't you come down now? I'll make you a fancy coffee and Kate'll feed you cake while I talk you into it. Five minutes?'

'Sam, I haven't even had breakfast yet!'

'Perfect. Nor have I. You can have a bacon roll *and* cake.'

He laughed and gave in, trying not to let himself get too excited by the idea of a place of his own. 'OK, but I need to tell Liv I'm not going back yet. I'll see you shortly.'

Sam was right.

The cabin was exactly what he needed, bigger than the studio flat he'd lived in for the past two years and right by the sea, as he'd been told. It didn't overlook the water, set down as it was behind the sea wall, but with the windows open he could hear it, and it was instantly soothing.

After he'd been introduced to Kate and the delightfully smiley Isadora, they'd settled down in their big sitting room with the sea stretched out in front of them as far as the eye could see, and eaten fat, juicy bacon rolls followed by cake washed down with copious coffee, and then Sam took him up onto the sea wall.

They strolled along to some railings and leant on them, listening to the soft suck of the sea on the shingle and watching the gulls wheeling over the water. 'Look at that—how can you resist it?' Sam asked with a grin, and Nick laughed.

'I don't even want to try. What sort of rent are

we talking about?' he asked, and Sam looked incredulous.

'What? You're the best friend I've ever had. Why the hell would I charge you money to stay here?'

'Because I'll be using electricity for heating and hot water, I'm invading your privacy—it's not fair.'

'It is fair. You can come sailing with me when I find a boat. Then I won't have Kate on my case about going out alone.'

He laughed and gave in. 'Well—if you're sure, and if Kate doesn't mind—'

'She doesn't. She really likes you. She says it'll be fun.'

He smiled at Sam. 'I really like her, too. You're well suited. How long have you known her?'

'Oh, not long. We met last January, but I didn't see her again until I started work here in April. Liv said you left in March, so I must have just missed you.'

'Yes, you must. So how does the maths work?' he asked, his mind ticking. 'Because Isadora's— what, five months old?'

Sam grinned. 'Yeah. Well, let's just say it was

love at first sight and leave it at that. Whatever, we couldn't be happier. So, when are you going to move in?' he asked, changing the subject, and Nick shrugged.

'I don't know, but to be honest I need to get out of there, for all sorts of reasons and the sooner the better. I'm working all week and I'm probably on call next weekend, but I'm not doing anything today, and Liv seems fine now. I could go and empty my flat and come straight back here tonight. Is that OK, or is it too soon?'

'No. Whenever. Makes no difference and if Liv's worried she can always call me. I'll give it a clean this morning, and you can have it as soon as you like. Do you need a hand with moving your stuff?'

'No, I'll be fine. I don't have a lot, it'll easily go in the car. And don't worry about sheets and towels, I've got all that.'

'Great. I'll give you the key now and then it's all yours.'

'How did you get on with Sam?'

He smiled fleetingly. 'Good. It was a bit weird going down to the harbour. I didn't realise how much I'd missed the sound of the sea—it sort of felt like I'd come home.'

There was something sad about the way he'd said that which tugged at her heartstrings. 'It could be home again,' she said, a little tentatively because she didn't want to push it, but he just nodded.

'Maybe. I hope so. The cabin's lovely, by the way, and Sam said I can have it as soon as I like, so I thought I'd go and empty my flat and move in there today, if you're feeling OK?'

He was moving out today? She'd thought—or maybe not thought, just hoped—that he'd stay a little longer.

'Yes—yes, of course, if it's what you want, but is there really that much of a rush?' she asked, curiously reluctant to let him go so soon. Or maybe at all? 'Why not leave it till next weekend? And what about Judy Richards?'

He was silent for a moment, then his eyes met hers fleetingly and flicked away again. 'Ben's going to keep an eye on her—he's on call this weekend anyway, and Sam says you can call him if you're worried or need anything. I'm working all week and I might be on call next weekend but I've got the opportunity today and I don't know when I'll get another one. And there's no rush, but now you're feeling better it might be wise for us not to be spending too much time alone together.'

'Wise?' Why *wise*?

'Yes. *Wise.*'

His eyes met hers again, and this time she saw the slow burn deep in the back of them, and heat flooded her body. She looked away hastily.

'I want you, Liv,' he said softly, 'but we're not ready for that yet. We need to take our time, be sure before we commit. And it's not as if we don't know how good it used to be.'

He was right, of course, but she felt a stupid surge of disappointment. 'So how about lunch, then, before you go?'

'Actually, I might just go now,' he said. 'We had bacon rolls and then Kate fed me a ton of cake so I really don't need to eat. Which reminds me, will you have enough food or do you want me to shop for you before I go?'

'No, it's fine, there's still some food in the fridge and I suspect the second your car's off the drive Gwen'll be round with a casserole or an apple pie to get the low-down anyway.'

He gave a wry chuckle. 'I don't know how you tolerate it.'

'Oh, they mean well, and I know it seems nosey but it's quite harmless. They're sweet, really, and they've been very kind to me.'

'Which is more than can be said for the hedge. He's tortured it into submission.'

She laughed, and once again his eyes caught hers and she saw the heat flaring in them. This time it was him who looked away.

'Are you sure you'll be all right if I go?'

'Nick, I'm fine. I'm better. I'm going back to work tomorrow.'

He frowned. 'Really? So soon? Are you sure?'

'Yes, I'm sure. I haven't even got a headache today. And I'll be fine. Go, get your stuff, get settled in. It's a good idea.'

He held her eyes for a second, then nodded. 'OK. Right, I'll get my bag,' he said. He ran upstairs, and she heard the slight creak of the boards as he went into the spare bedroom overhead, then moments later the stairs again as he came back down.

'That was quick.'

'I travel light. Don't get up. I'll let myself out.'

'No. I want to give you a set of keys before you go.'

She found them in the study—his study, in the top drawer of his desk—and handed them to him. It felt weirdly symbolic.

'So you can come and go whenever you want,' she said. 'No strings.'

He hefted them in his hand, met her eyes, his own unreadable again, and slipped them into his pocket.

'Thank you.'

'Don't thank me,' she said, shaking her head. 'I should be thanking you for looking after me—'

'It was my f—'

She cut him off, her fingers pressed over his lips. 'No. No more blame,' she said softly, and then she curved her hand around the back of his neck, drew his head down and kissed him.

For a second he froze, then his mouth softened, coaxing, tempting her until her lips parted to welcome him, his hand cradling her cheek as he deepened the kiss, tasting, searching, his tongue duelling with hers in a gentle, sensuous dance filled with promise.

Then he eased away, long before she was ready to let him go, opened the front door and turned on the step. 'Don't do anything rash, Liv,' he said gruffly. 'Don't forget you've got concussion. The signals in the brain can be disrupted for a month.'

'Nick, I'll be fine. Go. And ring me when you get back.'

He opened his mouth as if he was going to argue, then gave a rueful smile and nodded. 'Will do. Take care.'

And with a fleeting smile, he got into his car, fired up the engine and drove away.

She was on tenterhooks for the next twelve hours. Ridiculous, considering the number of times he must have been on the road in the last two years and she'd never given it a second thought.

It was different now. Now, she was letting herself care about him again, starting to forgive him—not for being unfaithful, because she'd done that long ago when she'd realised that she'd shut him out, but for letting her believe it all this time.

And she had to forgive herself, too—for making their lives a misery, for shutting him out, for putting him in a position where he'd been happy for her to think that he'd betrayed her trust because it gave him a way out of a situation that had become intolerable.

Why hadn't they talked? Because they were talking now. They'd done little else in the past forty-eight hours, and already the wounds hurt a little less.

Like the physical ones, from Friday. Every hour saw another patch of skin go black as the bruising came out, but it looked much worse than it felt and it really didn't hurt any more and nor did her head.

She pottered in the garden, tried a little weeding and gave up because bending over induced a headache and she didn't want to push it, even though her concussion had only been mild. Maybe Nick was right and she should take it easy.

Her phone pinged at midnight, with a text to say he was back at Sam's and see her tomorrow, and for the first time in hours she let herself relax.

Then on Monday morning just before eight, he rang her.

'Are you really coming in to work?'

'Yes, I am, but only light duties from nine to three. Are you still fretting about me?' she asked mildly.

'No, not at all, but I've put Judy on steroids. I've got a funny feeling about her—until we get the antiphospholipid result we won't know why she's had problems, but at least if the steroids have matured the baby's lungs it'll have more chance if we do need to deliver her in a hurry. I just thought you'd like to know.'

'Mmm. Thanks. Poor Judy. How is she?'

'Scared? She might appreciate a visit, if you've got a minute.'

She smiled. 'I'll drop in on her. And before you ask, no, I'm not driving, I'm going to walk in.'

'Good,' he said, sounding relieved. 'I'll see you later. Text me when you get here.'

So much for keeping their distance, she thought with a smile, but at least if they were at work there'd be no cosy moments to derail them.

* * *

To his surprise she walked onto the antenatal ward half an hour later, just as he went to check on Judy again.

'Gosh, two of you! It's like buses.'

'Mine's only a social call, Judy,' Liv said, turning towards her. 'I just popped up to say hi.'

'Oh! Your eye! What have you done?'

'Ah, yes. Minor accident on Friday.'

Nick snorted softly, and Judy glanced from him to Liv and back again, studying their nametags. 'You're both Jarvis,' she said slowly. 'Are you married, or is that just coincidence?'

He opened his mouth, looked at Liv and left it up to her.

'We were married—and no, he didn't hit me, it genuinely was an accident,' she said, and gave Judy a twisted little smile.

'Oh, gosh. Why did you let him go?'

Nick snorted again and picked up the board at the end of the bed, scanning her charts with half an eye while he waited for Liv to reply to that one.

'Yes. Bit silly, wasn't it?' she said eventually, and the silence grew a little awkward.

'Right, now we've established that I'm not a wife-beater, can we get back to business, please? Judy, how are you feeling?'

All trace of humour vanished from her face. 'Worried, if I'm honest, because there's something I didn't tell you that maybe I should have. I've been taking aspirin since just before I got pregnant.'

'Aspirin?' he asked, frowning, and glanced at Liv, who just shrugged and looked as stunned as he felt.

'Yes. I've been really worried about this APS thing but the test I had after my last miscarriage was negative so I thought I'd be all right, but then I read up about OAPS and it just seemed to fit, you know, and it said take aspirin, so I started taking it after my last period, and I don't know if it's coincidence but everything seemed to be going fine until I stopped—'

'You stopped? When?'

She nodded. 'About three weeks ago, because I was bruising so easily and I thought I might be doing more harm than good and I was a bit worried about having a haemorrhage, and it's all gone wrong since then.'

She pressed a hand over her mouth. 'It's my fault, isn't it? I shouldn't have stopped. I should have said something.'

'Yes, you should, because stopping it could certainly explain the baby's slow growth in the last few weeks,' he told her thoughtfully, 'but taking it could also have stopped you miscarrying in the first place, so, no, I don't think it was the wrong thing to do, but yes, you probably should have told us because had we known I would have put you back on aspirin on Friday as a precaution.'

'I'm so sorry—'

'No, don't apologise, Judy, it's OK, because I think it's just made everything a lot clearer, so here's what we'll do. I'm going to chase those results, because it's quite possible you *have* got obstetric antiphospholipid syndrome, which unlike normal APS only affects you when you're pregnant, hence the negative result before. Basically what happens is the blood clots in the capillaries in the uterine wall and can prevent implantation of an embryo, prevent the placenta developing, or cause it to fail later on, which may be what's happening with your baby now, but if that's what it is, it's utterly treatable and we can stop it in its tracks, so I'm going to put you back on aspirin just to be on the safe side, and we'll see what the results come up with and go from there. OK?'

She nodded, looking on the verge of tears. 'I'm sorry. I should have told you I'd been taking it, but I didn't want to look hysterical. I know doctors frown on people self-medicating.'

'There's nothing hysterical about it, Judy, and you may have done exactly the right thing. You've lost three babies already, but this one's still alive, and I'm going to make very, very sure that we do everything we can to keep it safe. OK?'

Her eyes filled, and she nodded. 'OK. Thank you.'

'My pleasure. Let's just hope we get some answers soon.'

Liv got to her feet. 'I'll leave you to it. I think there's a stack of filing with my name on it. I'll pop back and see you later if I get a minute, Judy.'

'That would be lovely.' Judy watched her walk away, then said, 'You ought to take care of her, she shouldn't be here, not with that eye,' and he met her reproachful eyes over the top of the charts and felt a twinge of guilt mixed with frustration.

'Tell me about it.' He sighed, and hung the charts back on the end of the bed. 'OK. I'll chase up the results, get you some aspirin and I'll be back later. Yell if you feel any different. They'll page me. And don't worry about Liv, I'm keeping an eye on her.'

'You do that. She's a lovely woman.'

As if he hadn't noticed.

He appeared in the ward office some time after she started sifting through the clearly non-essential paperwork, most of which needed shredding, from what she could see.

'Sorted Judy?' she asked, and he nodded.

'I wish she'd told us about the aspirin, I would have put her back on it prophylactically on Friday, but she's on it now and hopefully it won't be too late. Got time for coffee? I haven't had breakfast yet and I've been here since seven.'

'Yes, I've got tons of time,' she said with a wry smile, getting to her feet. 'Nobody will give me anything to do. I think they're all terrified by the black eye, so it's a good job they can't see my leg.'

'Probably, it was bad enough on Saturday and it can only be worse by now. Judy told me to take care of you, by the way, and said you shouldn't be here with that eye. I agreed with her.'

'Is that why nobody'll give me anything to do except filing, because you've been sticking your oar in?'

'I hardly needed to do that. One look at you is enough.'

She made a disgusted sound. 'Whatever, I'd like to kill whoever invented filing. I'm beginning to think it's possible to die of boredom and I've only been doing it for half an hour.'

He chuckled. 'I think you're trying to get out of a dull job.'

'Rumbled,' she said with a laugh, and they walked down to the café in a companionable silence.

He ordered their coffees and picked up a cereal bar and a banana. 'Want one?' he asked, waggling the banana at her, and she nodded.

'Yes, please. There wasn't much left in the

house so I only had toast for breakfast. Gwen didn't rock up with a casserole, by the way, but I did see her through the window and waved. I think the black eye might have scared her off.'

He winced. 'Perhaps you'd better explain about the accident before Bert comes looking for me with his garden shears.'

They found a table by the window, and he sat down and stretched his legs out. 'Before I forget, I put a food order in this morning so you'll have something for breakfast tomorrow. It should arrive at yours this evening between six and seven. I take it you'll be there?'

'You ordered food for me?' she said, puzzled.

'Yes. Well, some staples for you to save you having to shop, but I got some stuff for us to share, as well. I thought, if we're going to take this seriously and try and get to know each other again, maybe we should spend the evenings together when we can, and the kitchen in the cabin's a bit basic so I thought maybe we could do it at the house? I'll do all the cooking, so it should be easier for you, too. Unless you have any objections?'

'No, that sounds great. Why would I object

to being waited on? Did you order wine, by the way? I'm sorry I didn't have any over the weekend.'

'I don't drink any more,' he said. 'I still have the odd glass if I'm with friends, but I never buy alcohol routinely, and I absolutely never drink on my own. And I go to the gym, and I'm running again, and I've cleaned up my diet—too little, too late, but...'

He tailed off, leaving her to absorb all that for a second, and she shook her head.

'I thought you looked better,' she said quietly. 'Fitter. Healthier. More like the man I married—except you don't look like the man I married, because the man I married was happy, and you're not happy any more and that's my fault.'

'Liv, it's not your fault.'

'Yes, it is. I've destroyed your life, messed up your career, trashed everything, and I'm so sorry. I shouldn't have believed that you'd been unfaithful to me, because it was so unlike you, but when I thought about it, it didn't seem such a stretch to imagine that you'd turn to someone else, because you weren't showing any interest in me by then and I couldn't see what I had to offer you any longer. It was all so horrible—'

He gave a soft sigh, his voice quiet, his smile gentle, but he looked troubled, as if there was something he wanted to say. He didn't, though, just took her hand and squeezed it. 'Hey, no more, come on. This isn't the time or the place. Let's concentrate on the here and now—and right now, I'm operating in an hour and I haven't gone through the notes properly yet, so I'll take my coffee and go. You take it easy, I'll catch you later.'

She watched him go and sat there a moment longer, soaking up the sun, but then her phone rang, making her jump. It was Sam, checking up on her and asking if she felt she needed physio.

'No, Sam, I'm fine, but thank you. I'm back at work already.'

'Seriously? You've got concussion, not to mention the bruises.'

'Sam, I'm fine, really. And thank you for putting Nick up. It's very kind of you. He seems really happy with the cabin.'

'Good. You're welcome. Sorry, I've got to go,

I'm needed in Resus but you know where I am. Shout if you need anything and don't overdo it.'

The phone went dead, and she slipped it into her pocket, finished her coffee and went back to the tedious filing.

Overdo it? Chance would be a fine thing.

CHAPTER EIGHT

SHE WAS SENT down to cover for Jan again in the antenatal clinic after lunch, and Nick took one look at her and told her to go home. 'You're white as a sheet and you look shattered. Go on, out of here.'

'I'm fine. I'm only working till three. Don't fuss. How's Judy?'

'OK, but she has got antiphospholipid antibodies.'

'So she's definitely got OAPS?'

He gave a frustrated sigh. 'It looks like it, and I'm kicking myself for not putting her on aspirin on Friday when I admitted her. The more I think about it, the crosser I get.'

'Why? She'd already had a test that was negative, and Simon hadn't picked it up.'

'No, but his wife had just been diagnosed with cancer, so I doubt his mind was in the right place, and I wasn't firing on all cylinders either after finding we were working together, but two wrongs don't make a right.'

'No, they don't, but she'd withheld vital information, and anyway, it was a judgement call, Nick.'

'And I made the wrong judgement. Hence the expression "human error", but it's unforgivable when a baby's life's at stake. Still, I'd admitted her and she'd been monitored so we know nothing happened over the weekend. I suppose that's something to be thankful for. Right, Amy Zacharelli.'

She felt her eyes widen. It was Amy's baby he'd gone to deliver by emergency C-section on the day she'd thrown him out. Of all the coincidences...

'Amy's pregnant again already?'

'So it would seem.'

'Is she going for another section?'

'I don't know. I'm going to talk to her now I've seen her latest scan images. I'm hoping not. Simon's written "Query VBAC" in her notes, so it's obviously been discussed. Would you like to call her in?'

'Sure.'

She went out to the waiting room and called Amy, and a good-looking couple got to their feet. She'd never seen Amy, but she would have recognised Leo blindfolded. He was a celebrity chef, and she was a massive fan of his cookery show.

'May I come, too?' he asked with a coaxing smile, and she smiled back and hoped she didn't look too fan-girly.

'Of course, if Amy's happy. Mr Jarvis won't mind,' she said as she ushered them into the consulting room.

'Mr Jarvis?' Amy said, and her face lit up as she saw him in there. 'I thought you'd gone for ever.'

'So did I.' He got to his feet and smiled, shaking their hands. 'It's good to see you again, and not before time. I owe you both a massive apology. I promised to come back and make sure you were OK when I delivered your last baby, but I got caught up in something and then I was off on leave and I didn't even get a message to you. I'm really sorry.'

Caught up in something? On leave? One way of putting it when your wife calls time on your marriage, Liv thought, and wondered if she was the only person who could see what was going on under the surface of his calm, professional demeanour. She hoped so, for his sake, but both she and Nick were well aware that she'd found Suze's note while he'd been delivering Amy's baby.

'There's no need to apologise,' Leo was saying. 'I'm just sorry that we never had a chance to thank you, but I've never forgotten how kind you were to Amy, and how much we owe you.'

'You don't owe me anything,' Nick said, brushing it aside. 'It was a pleasure. So, how is your little girl? Is she doing well?'

'She's wonderful. Naughty, but wonderful,' Amy said with a laugh, 'and she's been fine, thanks to you and Mr Walker.'

'Do you know what this one is?'

'A boy,' Leo told him, his smile saying it all, and Liv felt the familiar shaft of pain like an old friend, but Nick's smile was convincing. If you didn't know better…

'Perfect,' he said. 'So, what are your birth plans? I see from your notes there's a suggestion you want to try for a normal vaginal delivery.'

'I want to, if I can. Mr Bailey said he was prepared to let me try, but he's apparently gone off on indefinite leave so I'm in the lurch again. I seem to have that effect on people.'

His smile was a little strained. 'I'm sure you can't take the blame for either of us abandoning you, but you're not in the lurch, unless I don't count? I'm replacing him for now, so I'll be looking after you for the rest of this pregnancy and I'm happy to let you try if everything looks OK.'

'You are?' Her face lit up, and she pressed her hands to her mouth. 'Oh, that's amazing! I was so worried, I thought his replacement might say no.'

'No. They're going to be close together, of course, only about fifteen months apart, but it's over a year so technically speaking that's not a problem. Why don't you hop up on the couch and let's have a look at your scar?'

All was well, he was relieved to see. The scar was a fine, tidy line, her uterus under the skin felt smooth, with only the slightest hint of a ridge over the incision site, and he could feel nothing to worry him.

'OK, Amy, I'm all done.' He snapped off his gloves and propped himself up on his desk. 'It's looking good,' he said. 'The head's engaged, everything looks fine, and I think I'll be quite happy to let you try. I'll make sure I'm here when you're admitted, but I don't see any reason why you shouldn't succeed. Liv?'

'No, I'd be happy to deliver you, Amy. I might be a bit less happy if it was a home birth, but provided you're here and we're keeping a close eye on things, I don't see a problem at all.'

'Oh, that's brilliant,' Amy said, tugging her clothes straight and picking up her bag. 'I feel so much happier now.'

He grinned at her enthusiasm. 'Good. I like my mums to be happy. I'll definitely make sure I'm around when you go into labour, and I'll do my best to give you the delivery you want, but the safety net is there. We'll make sure of that.'

'Thank you,' she said fervently, and then to his astonishment she went up on tiptoe and kissed his cheek. 'Thank you so much.'

'My pleasure. I'll see you in two weeks, if not before. I wouldn't want you to go over, but we'll see how it's going, and you might need a membrane sweep to chivvy things along, but so far, so good. You take care. It's good to see you both again.'

'You, too,' Leo said. 'Welcome back to Yoxburgh.'

Nick smiled and watched them go, wondering again what it would be like to come back here permanently, to see his patients extending their families, getting to know them over the years.

Maybe he'd get to find out?

He turned to Liv. 'Right, you, time to go home. I can manage the rest. They'll find me a nurse. Shoo. Go.'

She went, much more tired than she'd expected, and the short walk took her twice as long as usual. She let herself in and curled up on the sofa, her body tired and achy, her legs like lead. She'd just got settled when the doorbell rang, and she dragged herself off the sofa and opened the door.

Flowers.

Beautiful flowers, hand-tied and in a lovely vase, so she didn't even have to arrange them. There was a card, and she pulled it out of the envelope.

N xxx

Nothing more, but he didn't need to say more. His phone went straight to voicemail, so she left him a message thanking him, and spent the rest of the afternoon either dozing or staring at them with a silly smile on her face.

He cared. Still, after everything that had happened, he cared. And tonight couldn't come soon enough…

He looked tired but happier when he turned up, and although he'd shaved this morning she could see the dark shadow of stubble on his jaw again, and it sent a shiver through her.

He hugged her briefly, kissed her cheek and let her go, shoving his hands in his back pockets. To keep them out of trouble? Probably wise, she thought regretfully.

'So, did the shopping come?' he asked.

'Yes. And the flowers. They're beautiful. Thank you.'

'You're welcome. How are you?'

'Tired,' she admitted. 'I wasn't expecting to feel like this. It's not even as if my head aches.'

'Concussion's a weird thing. You need to take it easy. What about the rest of you?'

'All right. My bruises hurt if I touch them, but otherwise I'm fine.'

'Well, there's an easy answer to that,' he said with a grin.

He wandered through to the kitchen and started poking about in the fridge.

'So, what did you do this morning while I was filing?' she asked, following him.

'Oh, gynae surgery. All the usual stuff. Pretty dull. I like the babies.'

She laughed sadly. 'Me, too. We really chose the right careers, didn't we? So what do you reckon Amy Zacharelli's chances of delivering successfully are?'

'I don't know. She's due in sixteen days, but I don't want her to go over, really. It would be lovely if she went into labour spontaneously so we don't have to induce her but that could complicate things so I'm not holding my breath.' He pulled his head out of the fridge. 'How do you fancy a Thai chicken curry with cauliflower rice?'

She felt her eyes widen. 'That's a bit healthy. And I noticed everything's organic.'

'I told you I'd turned my life around. Too healthy?'

'No—no, it sounds great. Go for it. Can I do anything?'

'Yes. Sit down on the sofa there and talk to me while I cook.'

She turned her head and looked at it, squatting there in the 'family room' like a malevolent toad, taunting her with horrible memories.

'Do I have to?'

He looked up and met her eyes, and frowned. 'Hey, what's up?' he asked softly, abandoning the food and cradling her cheek in his hand. It was chilly from the fridge, and it sent a shiver down her spine.

'I don't like that sofa. Not since...'

'Oh, Liv.' Her name was a sigh on his lips, and he drew her gently into his arms and hugged her.

'Come on. We'll sit on it together and chase out the demons.'

And he took her hand and led her over to the sofa and sat her down next to him. 'There. See? It's just a sofa.'

She looked at the coffee table, and he followed her eyes and frowned. 'What's that mark?' he asked, leaning forwards and scratching at a dull, pale patch with his nail.

'You slopped your coffee when you stood up when I told you to go, and I put the paper under it to mop it up, and it stuck.'

He turned his head, his eyes shocked as they met hers.

'It's been there all this time?'

She shrugged. 'It didn't matter. I don't use it.'

He got up, found a sponge in the sink and came back, scrubbing at the stuck bits of paper until they dissolved and slid away. He gave the table one last swipe and straightened up to look at it.

'There, that's better,' he said, and bent and caught her chin in his fingers. 'Much better,' he added softly, and lowered his head the last few inches and kissed her. 'Now stay there, and I'll make you supper and you can talk to me.'

She looked at the mark, now nothing more than a slowly drying damp patch, and realised he was right. It was much better, in every way. Amazing what you could wipe away with a damp sponge…

She settled back into the corner, tucked a cushion behind her head and watched him cook while her lips tingled gently from his kiss.

'Thank you. That was amazing. I loved the cauliflower rice.'

They were back on the sofa, the one where her life had fallen apart last January, and he propped his feet up on the coffee table and rolled his head towards her.

'Don't get too addicted to it. I don't want you getting skinny again. You were way too thin, with all that running.'

'I know.' She looked away for a moment, and he caught her chin and gently turned her face towards him, his eyes searching.

'What?'

She shrugged, forcing herself to hold his steady gaze. 'I've wondered—you know, if that was why I never conceived?'

He dropped his hand and this time it was him who looked away. 'Not necessarily.'

She frowned. There was something he wasn't telling her, and she had a sinking feeling in her gut. 'Nick?'

He swallowed, sucked in a breath and let it go again slowly.

'I had semen analysis,' he said eventually, his voice heavy. 'Three years ago, after the second month you weren't pregnant.'

'And?' she prompted, her heart pounding. If they'd been trying for two years, and all that time he'd known—

'Well, I wasn't exactly firing blanks, but my sperm count was down on the optimum, and the quality wasn't stunning. It wasn't that bad, but it wasn't great, either.'

'So you cleaned up your act,' she said slowly, remembering how he'd suddenly stopped drinking wine and eating rubbish, rejoined the hospital gym, started running—but it hadn't lasted.

'Yes. And you still didn't get pregnant, and it was getting tougher and tougher, so I just let it all slide again. And then just before you found out you weren't pregnant, I had another test.'

Her heart thumped. 'And?'

'It was worse. Not catastrophic, but bad enough that it could definitely be an issue by then. I'd already decided that if you weren't pregnant I was going to talk to you, tell you the truth, but then when I got the result I was just numb, so I went to the conference, trying to work up the courage to tell you it was probably all my fault, and then Suze asked me what was wrong and I just lost it. And then when you thought I'd slept with her and kicked me out it seemed like the best idea because I thought if you hated me you'd find it easier to move on, but you haven't, and neither have I. But that's really why I didn't tell you the truth about Suze, because I didn't want you taking me back out of pity and going through endless cycles of IVF when you didn't really love me any more anyway.'

She slid her hand into his, threading their fingers together and holding on. 'I never stopped loving you, Nick.'

His fingers tightened. 'It felt like it, when you said you wanted a divorce. It felt as if you hated me, and I could see why, because I hated myself then and I thought if I got out of your life you'd find someone else and have babies the easy way, because IVF's tough, Liv. It can be really tough, I didn't know how tough until I saw others going through it, and you're younger than me, you've got years to find another man who can give you babies—'

'But I don't want another man, Nick, and I don't want anyone else's babies! I want you, and if it was right for us, down the line, I'd want *your* babies, via IVF or whatever other route we had to take so I could give them to you.'

She lifted her other hand and curled it round his jaw, turning his face back to her. 'That's why I never divorced you, because I love you,' she said softly. 'I'll always love you, and I couldn't bring myself to let you go.'

'Oh, Liv…'

He closed the gap between them, his mouth finding hers, sipping, searching, coaxing. She tipped back her head and his lips trailed down over her jaw, down her throat, over her collarbone until they met the soft, clinging fabric of her top.

And then he stopped, motionless for a moment

before he lifted his head and dropped the lightest, sweetest kiss on her lips and moved away.

'Don't stop.'

'I have to. We can't do this now, Liv. Not yet. Apart from anything else you're exhausted, you've had a long day and you need to go to bed.'

'So take me to bed.'

He gave a despairing little laugh and kissed her again. 'Nice try, but I need to go,' he whispered softly.

'I'll miss you.'

'I'll miss you, too, but it might be good for us. As they say, abstinence makes the heart grow fonder.'

She felt her mouth twitch into a smile, and she reached out and cupped his jaw again, her fingers testing the slight roughness of the stubble coming through. 'Promise me something.'

'What?'

'Keep the stubble this time? It makes you look sexy and a teensy bit badass.'

'What?' he said with a laugh. 'Why would you want me to look like that?'

'You know what I mean.'

'Yeah. Your bit of rough,' he said self-mockingly, and she smacked his hand and laughed.

'You are so not my bit of rough. It just makes you look—'

'Badass,' he said on a chuckle. 'Good grief. I don't want to upset my patients.'

'Too late to worry about that. You heard what Judy said about me letting you go. *She* thinks you're hot.'

He frowned and stared down at her. 'Hot? Judy? You're kidding me.'

She rolled her eyes, and he laughed again.

'Seriously?'

'You just have no idea, do you?' she said, shaking her head slowly from side to side. 'Nick, you are *such* a hottie.'

He lifted his hand, fingering his jaw thoughtfully. 'Well, maybe I should get a stubble blade for my razor. You know—just to keep you interested.'

His eyes were sparkling with mischief, and he looked so like his old self that it made her want to cry—or hug him. She did that, as the safest option, and then let him go.

'Go on, go home.'

'I wish,' he said softly, and she felt like crying again.

'I meant back to Sam's. Quick, while I'll still let you.'

He got to his feet and pulled her up, then kissed her again, his mouth lingering on hers for the longest moment before he took a step back out of reach.

'You go on up to bed. I'll put the dishwasher on and clear up before I leave. Shoo.'

She shooed, because she truly was exhausted, but she didn't sleep until she heard the front door close softly, and then the scrunch of tyres as he drove away. By the time the sound of his engine had faded, she was asleep...

He kept the stubble.

Not because of what she'd said, apparently, but because he had a call from the hospital about Judy Richards, so he'd thrown on his clothes and gone straight there.

By the time Liv went on duty at seven, he'd already been in the hospital for two hours and Judy had had another Doppler ultrasound scan of her placenta because the monitor had shown a slight dip in the baby's heart rate and it hadn't been moving quite as much as usual.

'Is she going to be all right?' she asked him, moving to stand next to him behind the nursing station desk, and he pursed his lips, his eyes still tracking over the scan images on the computer.

'I hope so. Her placenta's certainly not brilliant, but she's going to have another scan in two hours. If there's any change at all, I'm going to deliver it.'

'At thirty-two weeks?'

'Thirty-three today. And every day counts at this stage.'

He turned and gave her a tired smile. 'Talking of which, how are you?'

'Better. I slept like a log.'

'See? I told you you were tired,' he murmured.

'I'm not tired now,' she murmured, 'not looking at that badass stubble,' but he just laughed and stood up.

'No, you're at work,' he pointed out, but he winked at her as he turned away and her heart fluttered. Then he turned back.

'What are you doing this evening?'

'Eating with you?'

He smiled. 'Good. Want to come down to the cabin? I'll pick you and the food up, if you like.'

'Assuming Judy's OK, because I know you and I know she'll come first.'

'Are you jealous of a patient?'

She folded her arms. 'Absolutely.'

He laughed again and walked away, and she stood there staring after him like a moonstruck fool.

'You two seem to be getting on pretty well.'

She jumped and spun round.

'Ben! Do you have to sneak up on me like that? You scared the living daylights out of me!'

He raised his hands in apology. 'Sorry. I didn't mean to startle you, I just wanted your input on a patient,' he said, but his eyes were twinkling and she felt herself colour.

'No, you didn't, you were just fishing for gossip.'

'Not gossip. I'm actually very relieved to see you getting on, on several fronts.'

'Several?'

'Mmm. For a start you're alive, so after worrying us all to death on Friday that's a massive plus. And you're both friends of mine, so it's good to see you together again.'

'We're not "together" together, so don't get over-excited,' she cautioned. 'And anyway, that's only two fronts.'

'Well, he hasn't left yet, so we still have our locum. That's a very fat three.'

She chuckled. 'I can imagine. So, which patient did you want to talk to me about?' she asked, but he frowned thoughtfully.

'Patient? Did I say something about a patient?' he murmured, and then wandered off, leaving her laughing softly under her breath. *Idiot...*

'Liv, we've got a new mum on the way in in an ambo. Are you involved in a delivery at the moment?'

'No, do you want me to take her?' she asked the duty line manager, and she nodded.

'Please. The baby's OP, and she was in too much pain to get in the car, apparently. It's only precautionary, so it should be pretty straight-forward.'

Famous last words.

The back-to-back presentation was always potentially difficult, especially for a first-time mother, and the terrified young woman was in so much pain when she arrived that she refused to move, but without moving she was never going to get her baby out and it was ready to come.

'OK,' Liv said, 'I'll get you some pain relief, and then I'm going to get you up, because you're fully dilated and this baby needs you to push.'

'I can't—'

'Yes, you can, you'll see. I'll be back in a minute.'

She left the mother in the care of another midwife while she went to find Nick. 'Are you busy in the next half hour or so? I might need you.'

'Sounds promising,' he murmured, a lazy, sexy smile playing around his mouth, and she ignored the little shiver of need and rolled her eyes.

'I've got a primipara struggling with an OP labour and she might need a bit of assistance. I'm going to give her some Pethidine and then try and get her up, but I'm not holding out much hope. She's being pretty adamant about not moving.'

'OK. Page me if you need me. I've got a conference call with Ben's brother in an hour to talk about Judy's scans, but if I can help before then, give me a shout. Otherwise it'll be Ben.'

'OK.'

She didn't need him.

Between the painkiller, her partner's physical and emotional support and a bit of cajoling and encouragement from Liv, they got her up onto all fours which expanded her pelvis enough to allow the baby to pass through it, and no sooner was the mother lying down again with the squalling baby in her arms than there was a knock on the door and Nick stuck his head round.

'That answers that question, then,' he said with a crooked little smile. 'Everything OK?'

She smiled back, blinking away the tears that accompanied every delivery these days. 'Perfect, thank you, Mr Jarvis.'

'Good. Come and find me when you're done, please. I might need you.'

She raised an eyebrow, her back to the patient, and he winked and sent her blood pressure rocketing.

The door closed with a soft click, and she blinked again and turned back to the mother with what she hoped was a nice, professional smile firmly pinned on her face.

'You see?' she said. 'I told you you could do it. Well done.'

It was after seven before he finished work and came to pick her up. She didn't mind for herself, because she'd had a nap after she got home, but he'd been at the hospital for fourteen hours and he must be exhausted.

'How's Judy?'

'Fine. OK. Ben's brother Matt was pretty positive about the baby, which was good. It's handy having a prenatal paediatrician on tap like that. What do you fancy for supper?'

'Something quick and easy. You must be really tired.'

He smiled and dropped a kiss on her hair, hugging her gently. 'I am, but I need to wind down. I'm not on call tonight so I shouldn't get called in unless Judy has a crisis, and I'm hoping we've averted that, so I should get eight straight hours in bed.

'Fancy fish and chips?'

'I thought you were on a health kick?'

He laughed. 'It's not a health kick, it's a life-style choice, and I can choose to have a treat if I want one. Or if you'd rather, I can knock up a salad. I've got roasted aubergine, braised artichoke hearts, hot-smoked salmon fillets—'

'That sounds gorgeous.'

'Good. Right, let's go because the evening's ebbing away and we're wasting it and we both need an early night.'

He raided the fridge and drove her down to the harbour, pulled up outside the back of Sam and Kate's house and took her into the cabin.

'Oh, it's lovely!' she said, looking round. 'Really nice. And to think I was feeling sorry for you.'

'Oh, don't feel sorry for me, I'm very happy here, it's perfect. Or it is now, now you're here.'

He put the bag down and pulled her into his arms, staring down into her eyes and searching them for answers.

'Can we do this, Liv?' he asked softly. 'Can we make it work? Even if in the end we can never have kids?'

'We can give it our best shot. My mum this morning didn't think she was going to be able to get her baby out without help, but she did it.

Maybe that's the clue. Maybe we have to work at it instead of expecting it to look after itself. But you might have to feed me first,' she added with a smile as her stomach rumbled, and he laughed and let her go.

They had coffee after dinner with Sam and Kate, and they could see lights twinkling out on the water, and hear the clatter of the rigging from the boat yard, and she could see why Nick loved it so much.

Then Nick looked at his watch. 'Right, I need to get some sleep because until Judy's delivered I'm just waiting for the call.'

'You need to learn to delegate,' Sam said, which made her laugh.

'He doesn't delegate,' she told Sam. 'He doesn't trust anyone else—a little bit like you, really. I seem to remember you had to check up on me on Saturday morning after the accident.'

'Rumbled,' he said with a grin, and Nick pulled Liv to her feet.

'Come on, I need my bed. Thanks for the coffee, guys.'

'They're such nice people,' Liv said as he started the car. 'Have you told them about us?'

'No. I don't talk about us, you know that.'

'You talked to Suze.'

'Just once, and look where it got me.'

He gave her a fleeting smile, and even the moonlight picked up the sadness in his eyes.

He pulled up on the drive and cut the engine.

'Oh. Are you coming in?' she asked. 'I thought you were in a hurry to get to bed?'

That made him chuckle. 'Are they mutually exclusive?'

Her jaw dropped a fraction and he stopped teasing her. 'If I kiss you goodnight out here in the car the way I want to kiss you goodnight, Bert and Gwen will probably have a stroke.'

She stifled a laugh and opened her door. 'Well, we can't have that.'

'Absolutely not.'

He followed her into the house, still chuckling, closed the door and leant back on it, pulling her into his arms.

'Oh, that's better.' His mouth found hers, and he felt the smile on it fade as need moved in and swamped them both.

She arched up and kissed him back, tunnelling her fingers through his hair as he plundered her mouth, his hands holding her head steady as he deepened the kiss, his tongue duelling with hers, his hips rocking against her body.

Then he lifted his head and rested his forehead against hers, his breath rasping in and out as if he'd been running.

'I want you,' he whispered roughly, nipping and nibbling over her throat as she arched her head back invitingly.

'So stay,' she murmured, and he wavered for a second then shook his head.

'No, I can't. I have to go. I'm dead beat and I'm on call tomorrow night, so this is my last chance at a good uninterrupted stretch. What time are you on tomorrow?'

'Seven, again.'

'Me, too. I'll pick you up at a quarter to, and we can have breakfast together when I've done my ward round if you're not involved in a delivery by then.'

He kissed her again, just a tender, lingering caress, and then he moved her gently out of his way before he surrendered to temptation. It would be so easy—

'I need to go.'

'I know you do. I love you.'

He groaned. 'Oh, Liv. I love you, too,' he murmured. He kissed her again, then opened the door, got into the car and drove away, wondering what the hell he was doing and why, when he could have been upstairs with her by now, buried in that beautiful, willing body.

He must be mad, but he was also wary and he didn't want to be hasty.

Yes, he loved her, and he needed her, and she clearly felt the same way, but there was so much left unresolved about their infertility, so many things they hadn't tried. They'd hardly got past first base, but their relationship had already crumbled under the strain and he wasn't sure he could face the emotional upheaval of trying to repair their marriage, just to watch it torn down again.

He just had to be sure when they took that next step that they were doing it for all the right reasons, and that meant going back to his own bed.

Alone—but hopefully not for much longer, because the waiting was killing him.

CHAPTER NINE

'YOU'VE GOT STUBBLE RASH.'

His finger traced her top lip, and she had to resist the temptation to draw it into her mouth and suck it. In the hospital café, right in front of everyone, that might not be smart.

'Stop frowning, you'll get wrinkles,' she told him.

'Good. It might stop the patients thinking I'm hot, of all things,' he said, sounding almost disgusted with himself. 'I can't believe I scraped your lip with my stubble.'

She chuckled. 'Well, if you will kiss me like that…'

'Then I'll have to shave. And I fully intend to kiss you like that. Every night. At least.'

She didn't even try to stop the smile. 'Good. How's Judy?'

'Fine. Stable. Her placenta seems to be holding its own and I'm going to get another ultrasound to check if the baby's grown at all. If not, I might have to reconsider leaving her any longer.'

He glanced at his phone. 'Right. I'd better get on.'

'Me, too.' She drained her coffee and walked back towards the maternity unit with him, parting at the lift.

'Lunch?' he asked.

'If I'm free. What are you doing now?'

'I've got my first stint in the fertility clinic.'

She felt her heart hitch in her chest.

'Have fun,' she said lightly, but just the word *fertility* was enough to bring all her fears home to roost. Were they really ready to go back to all that?

'Send me a text when you finish. Failing that, supper?'

'Sounds good. I'll catch you later.'

They fell into a routine from then on.

He picked her up from home if their shifts started at the same time, and if not she walked in, not because she shouldn't drive yet after her concussion, but just because the weather was warmer now and so beautiful and she enjoyed it.

If they could, they shared a break, and if their shifts allowed, they ate together in the evenings, and when they couldn't do either and they weren't working together, he sent her texts. Sometimes cheeky, sometimes funny, sometimes just simply, 'Miss you'.

And bit by bit, over the course of the next week, they started to relax with each other and have fun. And he kissed her. A lot.

And then he rang her at six on Thursday morning, nearly two weeks after her accident, to tell her that Amy Zacharelli was on her way in.

'I'd like you to be her midwife, if that's possible. I think you're on at seven, aren't you?'

'Yes, I am. That's fine, I'll come in now and sort it with my line manager. Don't worry, I'll be there.'

'Good. I'll see you shortly. I'll make sure she's in a side room in the labour ward.'

'OK. Thanks. See you.'

She had the fastest shower on record, grabbed a banana out of the fruit bowl and ate it on her walk in. No time to think about driving, or parking the car, so she walked briskly and arrived just as Leo pulled up at the entrance with Amy.

'Hi, Amy,' she said as Leo opened the door. 'Nick's here, we're all ready for you. Are you OK to walk?'

'I'll be fine, but Leo has to park the car.'

'That's OK, I'll stay with you and check you in. Leo, do you want to park and come back and find us? We'll be on the labour ward on the fourth floor.'

'Sure. Thanks.'

He got back in the car and drove off, and Amy grabbed her hand and held on. 'Oh. Contraction.'

'That's OK. Just relax and breathe through it, there's no hurry. You can lean on me if it helps.'

The next one was three minutes later, just as they arrived on the ward, and the third one came as Leo walked in through the door. She sent Nick a text, and he must have been in his office because there was a tap on the door and he was there just as Amy was undressing, so she slipped out to update him.

'How's it going?'

'Contractions every three minutes, dead on. I haven't had time to examine her yet so I don't know how dilated she is, but so far she's coping well. I don't know what you want to do about pain relief?'

He pulled a face. 'Nothing if she can manage without it, and I'd really rather she didn't have an epidural because she won't have any feedback if her uterus starts to tear along the scar, which she would feel otherwise. Has she asked for pain relief?'

'No, not yet. I just wanted all my ducks in a row.'

'Well, see how it goes. Don't let her struggle.'

'I won't. I'll put her on a monitor in a minute. Do you want to examine her yourself or do you want me to do it?'

'No, you do it, it's your labour. I'm just on standby,' he said. 'I'll come in and say hi, and then leave her with you.'

'Sure? That sounds like delegating,' she teased.

He laughed softly, checked the corridor and dropped a fleeting kiss on her lips. 'Of course I'm sure. I trust you.'

'OK. I'll leave her with you while I get rid of my stuff and tell them I'm here, then I'll be back.'

She was only two minutes, and she found Amy

propped up on the bed, with Leo perched on the edge. Nick had put her on the monitor, and the baby's heart rate was nice and steady.

'Good, you're back,' he said, his eyes speaking volumes. 'She could do with a quick check, I think.'

AKA things are moving rapidly. She nodded and snapped on some gloves. 'If you hang on I'll give you a progress report,' she murmured and turned to Amy. 'Right, let's have a look. How are you doing?'

'OK, I think. I wasn't expecting it to hot up so quickly.'

'Everyone's different,' she said comfortingly. 'Still happy to give this a try?'

'Oh, yes. I don't want another C-section, not with two little ones to look after.'

'Well, we'll try and avoid it, but if you start getting any sharp or persistent pains around your scar area that aren't like the contractions, tell us straight away. I'll just examine you and see how far on you are.'

'OK—oh, it's another one.'

'Two minutes,' Nick murmured in her ear, and she nodded as her eyes flicked to the monitor.

'Right, try and relax, let your body do the work. That's it, you're doing really well.'

She watched the baby's heart rate dip a fraction, then recover as the contraction eased. 'OK now?'

Amy nodded and leant against Leo, who was sitting up beside her pillows, his arm around her shoulders.

'Right, Amy, can you just drop your knees out for me and relax as much as you can—that's lovely—wow, you're doing really well. You're nearly there. There's just a tiny anterior lip of your cervix left to pull up and you're ready to go.'

'Really? So fast?'

Liv pressed the call button to summon another midwife. 'Like I said, everyone's different and your baby's obviously in a hurry.'

'I need to push now!' she said, her eyes widening, grabbing Leo's hand.

'Well, that answers that,' she said with a smile. 'Just pant for me, Amy. Don't push until I'm sure that lip's gone.'

'Do you mind if I stay?' Nick asked, and she glanced over her shoulder at him, her smile slipping a fraction. He was such a sucker for a new baby.

'Be my guest,' she said softly. 'There should be two of us and nobody's come yet. Right, let's have a look—OK, it's gone, so on the next contraction I want you to take a deep breath and tuck your chin down and push for me.'

'Can I move? I sort of want to kneel, I think.'

'Sure. Turn round and lean on Leo, or the pillows, whatever's most comfortable.'

'Shall I glove up?' Nick murmured. 'They're pretty busy.'

'If you don't mind.'

His smile was crooked. 'When did I ever mind being present at a delivery?' he asked, and turned away before she could answer.

'Oh, I have to push!'

'OK. Deep breath, chin down, let your breath out as you push into your bottom—that's lovely. Good girl. Well done.'

Two contractions later the baby's head was crowning, and Liv told Amy to pant as she carefully guided the baby's head out and round and checked for the cord.

'Right, little push for me—perfect, well done!'

Amy turned and sat down, and Liv stood back and let Nick lift the baby and pass him to Amy, the tiny slippery body safely cradled in those big, capable hands.

He looked so sure, so natural, so perfect…

He glanced up and met her eyes, and she had to turn away. He wanted this so much for them, needed it so much, and she realised in that moment that she'd go through anything to give him a child.

But what if it never happened for them? What if they went through all the intrusive and gruelling procedures that could be tried and still got nowhere? Would they be able to cope?

She heard the snap as he pulled off his gloves, then felt his arms come round her in a gentle hug.

'Well done, my love,' he murmured, and she knew they had to try, even if they failed, because not to try was to condemn them both to eternal regret.

Nick stayed just long enough to congratulate them and make sure all was well, then retreated to his office, shut the door and leant back against it with a shaky sigh.

Why did he do this job? He must be a masochist.

And Liv thought working in the fertility clinic was hard for him? He let out a humourless little laugh. Every time he saw a baby born, his heart tore a little more. Delivering babies, handing them to their delighted parents—that was far harder, knowing how out of reach it was to him and Liv.

Sure, it was a wonderful and joyous thing to do, but on a personal level it killed him a little bit more every single time—and watching Liv, he knew she felt it, too.

There was a tap on the door behind him, and he took a deep breath, blinked away the tears he hadn't even known were there and opened the door.

'Hi, Ben. What's up?'

'Nothing, I just saw that Amy Zacharelli's come in. I wondered if you knew.'

'Yes, she's had the baby, I was there,' he said, and turned away, flicking through a file on his desk because he wasn't sure his feelings weren't written all over his face. 'Straightforward easy delivery, mum and baby both doing well. I left them in Liv's hands. She knows where I am.'

'Good. Great.'

There was a pause, and Nick frowned and turned back to look at Ben. 'Was there something else?'

'How are you and Liv?'

He blinked. 'What's that got to do with the price of fish?'

'That's not a straight answer to a straight question.'

He shut the file and forced himself to meet Ben's eyes.

'I didn't think it was a straight question. I would say it was thoroughly loaded and probably none of your business.'

Ben studied him thoughtfully for a moment, then nodded slowly. 'OK, fair enough, but it's kind of relevant. Off the record, Simon's not coming back. Jen's doing OK, but he says it's going to be a long haul and whichever way it goes, they need to be near the family for support, so I'm going to have to advertise the post. I'm going to be blunt, I want you back but only if you and Liv are OK with it. You fit in well, you know your way around, you're a team player, you have additional skills which we need—we don't need to look any further, but I need to know that you're going to stick around if we appoint you. Assuming we do appoint you, which I think is pretty much a given, but we have to abide by the rules and advertise.'

His heart was thumping in his chest, because a part of him wanted this so much it was eating him alive. The other part was still wondering if he and Liv stood a prayer of making it work.

'Of course you have to advertise it. And you don't know what that'll throw up. You might get someone extraordinary apply.'

Ben shrugged. 'We might, although I doubt very much we'd get anyone better than you, but the bottom line is I can't even consider you for the post if you and Liv are going to find you can't hack it, because that's no good for either of you and it's no good for the department. I need to know that you're in it for the long haul.'

He couldn't give Ben an answer. Not yet, not without talking to Liv.

'You said it's off the record.'

'You can talk to Liv. She's the soul of discretion and anyway, her support is key. I realise that.'

He nodded. 'OK. Thanks for the heads up. I'll let you know. When's the closing date?'

Ben laughed. 'Realistically, until we get a suitable candidate, but probably a month at the outside? If you don't apply, we'll have to keep the advert open until we get someone. Talk to Liv, think it over. I don't want to put you under pressure.'

That made him laugh.

'Yeah, right,' he said drily, then shook his head slowly. 'Leave it with me, Ben. I knew it was a possibility, but I hadn't really let myself consider it, so this is a bit of a game-changer.'

'No hurry. This needs to be the right decision.'

He nodded again, but didn't say any more because there wasn't really anything to say. Not until he'd spoken to Liv, and he wouldn't do that until they could talk about this properly, in private.

Leo, Amy and baby Rocco left the hospital at three, just at the end of Liv's shift.

To her surprise Nick came to say goodbye, and Leo put the baby carrier down and hugged them both.

'Thank you so much. I'm so, so grateful. So's Amy.'

'Absolutely,' Amy chipped in. 'I can't believe I didn't need a section, I really didn't think it was going to happen. I'm so glad you let me try, and that you were both there. It made me feel so safe, and that made a massive difference, and so has not having had a section. I couldn't have done it without you, either of you.'

Tears welled in her eyes, and Liv hugged her gently and told Leo to take her home. 'Go on. Go and show the girls their little brother. I'm sure they'll be thrilled to bits.'

'I'm sure they will,' Leo said, his smile a little crooked. 'I know we are. Look, I don't know if you like eating out, if it's your thing, but if you want to come down for dinner to the restaurant any time, just phone up and we'll find you a table. It would be great to see you again.'

'That's very kind of you, Leo, thank you.'

'It's nothing,' Leo said. 'Remember, any time.'

'That would be lovely,' Liv said, reaching up

and kissing Leo on the cheek. 'Thank you. Now take your wife home, please, and spoil her a little. She's done really well today.'

They watched them go, Leo with one arm round Amy and the other carrying their precious cargo, and Liv felt Nick's hand on her shoulder, giving it a quick squeeze.

'You did well today, too,' he murmured. 'Thank you for coming in early.'

'You don't need to thank me, Nick. I did it for Amy. I knew she'd feel better with people she knew around her, especially under the circumstances. That's all the thanks I need.'

'I'm still thanking you. What are you doing later?'

'I don't know. Are you going to tell me?' she asked, looking up and catching a fleeting glimpse of worry in his eyes. 'Nick? What is it?'

His hand dropped from her shoulder and he shook his head. 'Nothing. Nothing to worry about, but there's something we need to discuss and we can't do it here. Yours or mine?'

'Come to the house. I need to put some laundry on and I could do with washing my hair. I didn't have time this morning. What time do you finish?'

He laughed. 'How long is a piece of string? Hopefully by seven anyway. Judy's OK, so I'm starting to relax on that front, and I haven't got any other mums I need to worry about at the moment—well nothing urgent anyway. I'll give you a call if I get held up but you should probably eat without me to be on the safe side.'

'OK. I'll see you later.'

It was much later.

He rang at six to say that Judy's blood pressure had risen suddenly and the Doppler scan of her placenta showed marked deterioration.

'You weren't worried earlier. Famous last words?' Liv said, knowing what was coming next, and he gave a tight laugh.

'You could say that. Anyway, I'm going to have to deliver the baby and I know I'm not supposed to be here tonight but I promised her I'd look after her and after we've got her this far I'm not going to let her down.'

'Of course you're not, you old softie. Get something to eat before you take her into Theatre, and I'll see you later, maybe.'

'OK, but don't hold your breath. I might have to take a raincheck.'

'OK. That's fine. Just let me know.'

She put the phone down, examined the contents of the fridge and decided to make a Thai chicken curry with cauliflower rice. She knew he liked it, she had all the ingredients and he could reheat it when he got there or she could freeze it.

It didn't take long, and after she'd eaten hers the evening seemed to stretch out endlessly. There was nothing she wanted to watch on the TV, she still hadn't washed her hair, and she really fancied a nice, long, lazy bath.

Probably with a glass of wine, but there wasn't any in the house, so she made a fruit tea and took it up with her, ran the bath, added bubbles and found her book before climbing in.

Luxury.

She wallowed until the bubbles had all gone, the water was tepid and her book was all but finished, then pulled out the plug, washed her hair in the shower and dried it.

Did she bother to dress, or should she just put on her towelling robe and slippers and assume he wasn't coming? Probably a safe assumption. She could lie on the bed and finish her book while she waited.

By the time she'd turned the last page there was still no word from him, and it was after ten. She might as well just go to sleep.

The house was in darkness, apart from a light in the hall.

Should he go in? He really needed to talk to her, but she wasn't at work tomorrow so he wouldn't see her then, and Ben's words were gnawing at him.

And she'd given him keys.

He let himself in, and swore as the alarm started its entry countdown. He flipped down the cover on the control panel and punched in his old code on autopilot, but it carried on beeping, the seconds ticking down. 'Dammit, of course, she's changed the code—'

The alarm gave up waiting and wailed into life, and he frantically keyed in the new number and sighed with relief as it went quiet. Not before the light went on in Bert and Gwen's house, though. Damn. That was all he needed.

'It's only me,' he called, as their front door opened.

'Is everything all right?'

'Yes, it's fine, Bert. No problem. Sorry to disturb you.'

He shut the door as Liv appeared at the top of the stairs, hastily belting her robe, her hair tousled. 'I'm sorry, I shouldn't have set it but you didn't ring. Was Bert cross?'

'No, worried I think. I expect he thought I'd broken in to give you another black eye.'

She laughed and shook her head. 'No, they know I was knocked down by a car. I told them.'

'Well, thank God for that, I thought he was about to call the police. And I'm sorry I didn't ring you. I thought I'd left it too late, but I just needed to talk to you, and then I saw the hall light on and I thought you might still be awake.'

'Oh, that's my fault as well, I must have forgotten to turn it off.' She ran lightly down the stairs and kissed his cheek. 'Have you eaten? I made a Thai curry for us and there's some left.'

'That sounds amazing. I grabbed a piece of toast from the ward kitchen but that was hours ago.'

'Come and eat, then, and you can tell me all about Judy.'

'She's fine, and the baby's fine,' he said, following her into the kitchen. 'Small, but pretty well. She's in SCBU but she's over thirty-four weeks so it's not too much of a worry. She'll just need a bit of support.'

'Well, that's good. I bet they're really happy.' Liv took a bowl out of the fridge and put it in the microwave and turned to him with a concerned smile.

'So what was it you wanted to talk to me about?'

He hesitated, then went for it. 'Simon's not coming back,' he said, studying her face for her reaction. 'Ben wants me to apply for the job, but there was a sort of caveat that I'm not going to do another runner.'

'And are you?'

He sighed heavily. 'I don't know, Liv. It all depends on you and the baby thing. If we jump through all the available hoops, have every test, go through every procedure and still fail, will you be to deal with it?' he asked softly.

'Yes—because we love each other, and we'll be all right.'

'Sweetheart, you don't know that. I've seen level-headed, reasonable people take each other apart over this, and it's not because they don't love each other. Look what happened to us before.'

She hitched up onto the stool beside him. 'But we weren't talking. We'd stopped communicating with each other—you didn't even tell me you'd had semen analysis, for goodness sake! We should have shared that right at the beginning, when you had the first test, talked about the result and what it meant.'

'But I didn't *know* what it meant. I didn't know if it was bad enough to make a difference, so I tried to improve it, I changed my lifestyle—'

'And it still didn't work, so instead of talking to me and sharing your fears you shut me out. How much of an improvement was that?'

He stabbed a hand through his hair.

'It wasn't. I know that. But I felt guilty—'

'That's ridiculous, it wasn't your fault—'

'It was my fault, or it could have been. You're right, I should have talked to you about it when I had the first test, never mind the second. But I didn't, because I couldn't, because it was falling apart all around us and we weren't talking about anything by that point.'

'Oh, Nick. Come here...'

Her arms slid round him, and he turned on the stool and took her in his arms, resting his cheek against her hair. It smelt of sunshine and apples and Liv, and he buried his face in it and breathed deeply. He wanted her so much. Needed her so much.

'I just feel—this is a real chance for us, Liv, but I can't muck Ben around, so I have to tell him yes and stick with it or give up on us and get another job somewhere else.'

'You can't do that!' she said, her voice a desperate whisper. 'You can't walk out on us now, Nick. Please? I love you. I need you. And you said you needed me.'

His arms tightened round her. 'I do, more than anything else.'

'So apply for it. From the way Ben's talking, it's yours for the asking, so ask. We know we can work together. If we find we can't live to-gether, then we'll deal with it.'

'You make it sound so easy, but it's not. It's the job I always wanted, the job I'd just secured when we split up. I'm lucky he's even giving me a second chance at it, and I'm so, so tempted, but—he wants me to be able to commit to some-thing I just don't know the answer to and I don't want us to feel trapped. We felt trapped before and it nearly killed us.'

She pushed herself away so she could look up at him, and he met her eyes, open, honest, and so revealing.

'We won't feel trapped,' she promised him. 'Not this time, because this time we'll be going into it with our eyes open. Have you told him about us? About the baby thing?'

'No. That's why I went private for the semen analysis. You know what the grapevine's like.'

'Don't you think you should tell him?'

He swallowed hard. 'They're just about to have their third child. His fourth.'

'So? It's not a competition.'

'It feels like it sometimes—and you know that. It's why you wouldn't come to the conference.

Anyway, it's none of his business and it's not relevant to whether or not I can do the job, so he can't legally use it as a reason for not offering it to me.'

He sighed and rammed a hand through his hair.

'The trouble is I just feel I don't have a choice. There aren't any other decent jobs out there and that's taken away any choice over whether or not I apply for this one because I need a job, one way or the other, or I can't pay the mortgage and you'll be homeless. We'll be homeless. I can't do that to you.'

'You can't do this just for money, Nick, and I won't let you! I could pay the mortgage—or rent something, if it came to that. If we want to be together and can accept the fact that we might never have children, and I think we both feel like that, then we should be together, either here or somewhere else. Anywhere, so long as we were happy, but you can't take this job just because you need to earn a living. It has to be because it's what you really, truly want, and only you can decide that.'

He reached out a hand and rested it lightly

against her cheek, over the faint yellow stain left by the bruise. He frowned and traced the stain tenderly with his thumb.

'It is what I really, truly want,' he said softly. 'That, and you, as a package. But you first. Always you, front and centre.'

A frown pleated her brow and her eyes were troubled. 'Then what's the problem? Life doesn't come with guarantees, and Ben knows that, but you're talking as if you're expecting it to go wrong between us. It can't work with that attitude. We both have to be behind it one hundred percent, or it won't work. It can't work.'

'I am behind it,' he said. 'I was behind it before, and look what happened.'

Her hand caressed his face, her fingertips gentle against his cheek. 'Yes, look what happened. We didn't talk, we didn't say "I love you", we didn't take care of each other. We just let everything between us grind to a halt because I didn't get pregnant. And we won't do that this time. We *can't* do that this time, because that's not what it's about. It's about the fact that we love each other and want to be together, and we can't let that fail, so why don't we just kick this baby thing into the long grass and concentrate on *us*? Because I miss you, Nick, I miss you *so* much.'

His fingers stroked her cheek tenderly, sliding down to cup her chin as he shifted towards her and touched his mouth to hers in a gentle, lingering kiss.

'I miss you, too,' he murmured gruffly. 'And you're right, we can't let it fail this time. We'll give it everything we've got, no holding back. But on one condition. This baby thing—I don't want to think about it or worry about it until we're feeling confident and settled and we know we're strong enough to face it. I'm almost one hundred percent sure that we'll need help in some form or another, and I don't want to start down that road until we're both sure we're ready. If we ever are.'

She nodded slowly. 'I'll buy that. It's a good idea.'

He kissed her again, the caress tender and sensuous, the passion reined in. But it was there in her, too; he could feel it simmering just below the surface, ready to explode at the slightest provocation, so he drew back.

She curled her fingers over his jaw and let

her fingers explore the texture. He could feel his stubble catching on her skin, grazing softly against it, and her pupils darkened.

'You didn't shave today,' she murmured.

He felt her smile against his lips and drew away again. 'No, I didn't have time, and anyway, you said you liked it.'

'I do.' She smiled back and leant in again, kissing him once more, her fingers still curled softly against his jaw. 'Stay with me,' she murmured, and he felt his pulse hammer in his throat. Could she feel it? Probably.

He turned his face into her palm and kissed it, then got to his feet. 'Not tonight. Not when I'm exhausted. I need some sleep, Liv, and so do you. I'll see you tomorrow and we'll talk then.'

'Stay anyway,' she said suddenly. 'You can use the spare room if you don't want to share ours. You've already slept in there, it's not like I've got to find clean sheets for you. I might even bring you early morning tea.'

'No, Liv, I'm going to Sam's. I'll ring you in the morning.'

He cradled her head in his hands and kissed

her lightly on the lips, then forced himself to let her go. 'Sleep well. I'm sorry I woke you.'

'You, too. And, Nick? Don't worry. It'll be all right.'

CHAPTER TEN

HE KISSED HER AGAIN, then let himself out, and she listened as he started the car and drove away.

Would they really be all right? She could only hope, because that was all she had left, but at least she *had* hope now. It was more than she'd had for ages, that and determination, and she was going to do everything in her power to make this work.

If he applied for the job and didn't get it for some reason then they'd go elsewhere, because one thing she was sure of, she wasn't losing Nick again, come what may. She'd live in a hut delivering babies in some third-world country so long as she was with him.

She went back into the kitchen to turn off the lights and realised he hadn't had the curry. Poor Nick. He'd be eating toast again, but it was too late now. She threw it out, set the alarm again and went up to bed.

* * *

Nick made himself some toast—again—and went to bed alone, racked with frustration and buoyed up by hope.

He'd been so tempted to stay with her, so tempted to scoop her up in his arms and carry her up to bed, but he wanted it to be better than that, better than some random fumble when he was reeling with exhaustion and running on empty.

No. If they were going to make a success of it, they needed a clean slate, and that meant taking it all back to first principles.

A first date to remember…?

He could take her to Zacharelli's. Leo wouldn't have had time to speak to them by tomorrow, but he might get lucky with a cancellation—or, failing that, there'd be somewhere else he could take her to and spoil her.

And then he'd bring her back here.

Sam and Kate were away for the weekend, they'd have the place to themselves—and neither of them was working on Saturday, either, so they could get up when they wanted, or stay in bed all day. No prying neighbours, and even more importantly, no ghosts from their tortured past. No echoes of sadness, no blighted memories, just the two of them alone together with a clean slate.

Less than twenty-four hours and she'd be here with him, in his arms.

The wait was going to kill him.

'Do you have any plans for tonight?'

She cradled the phone in one hand and carried on sorting washing with the other. 'No—I thought you were coming over?'

'I am. I'm taking you out for dinner. We've got a table at seven-thirty. Wear something pretty.'

Her heart jiggled happily in her chest. 'Are you taking me on a date, Mr Jarvis?'

'I am, Mrs Jarvis. I most certainly am.'

'How posh?'

'Oh, nice but not that posh. Smart casual?'

She smiled. Nick did smart casual like no other man she'd ever met. 'Perfect.'

Except it wasn't, of course, because she didn't have anything in her wardrobe that fitted any more that could come under the heading of smart casual. She hadn't had any need for it until now—unless…

She opened her wardrobe and pulled out a subtle blue-grey dress that hadn't seen the light of day for over two years. It had a soft metallic sheen, the fabric almost fluid, and she'd given up wearing it because it hung on her after all the running, but Nick had always loved it because it exactly matched the colour of her eyes.

And, she remembered, he could take it off easily.

A secret little smile on her face, she stripped and pulled it on, and it fitted perfectly again now she was a sensible weight. And she had some ridiculously high heels that were covered in tiny sparkly bits—nothing casual about them, but Nick was a sucker for high heels and she hadn't been able to resist them.

But he'd said they were going for it, holding nothing back, so—underwear? She tugged open the drawer and found nothing that was other than practical and utilitarian. She'd hadn't bought sexy underwear for ages, but she was going to today, and when she'd done that she'd see if she could get a manicure and pedicure. Nick always found painted toenails a turn-on.

Fizzing with excitement, she hung the dress up, pulled on her jeans and a jumper, and went shopping.

She was wearing that dress.

His pulse shot up, and he had to take a deep breath and count to ten. Twenty when he clocked the shoes.

'How do I look?'

'If we didn't have a table booked, I'd slam the front door and carry you upstairs and to hell with everything,' he said tightly, 'but we do, so let's not talk about how you look, eh?'

She smiled the smile he hadn't seen since the day after her accident, and he leant in and kissed her cheek. Her signature perfume wafted over him, and he sucked in his breath and pulled away.

'You look beautiful, Liv. Come on, let's go.'

'Is it far? Only the shoes aren't very practical to walk in.'

He laughed softly and shook his head as he

settled her coat on her shoulders. 'No. No, it's not far, but we're taking the car anyway.'

'So where are we going?' she asked as he pulled off the drive and headed towards the sea front.

'On a need to know basis...'

'Nick, tell me!'

'No. It's a surprise.'

'We're not—no, we can't be...'

She trailed to a halt as he pulled up beside the prom, backed into a space and cut the engine.

'Yes, we can. I rang this morning, and Leo has already spoken to his staff.'

'But—it takes months to get a table! It's got two Michelin stars, Nick, for heaven's sake! It'll cost a fortune.'

'I know, and guess what? It's worth every penny just to have you beside me again. This is our first date, Liv. The first mark on our clean slate. Ready to rewrite history?'

The smile lit up her face. 'Absolutely. What a perfectly wonderful idea.'

She reached for the door handle.

'Uh-uh. Wait for me.'

He got out, went round and opened the door,

and she stepped out onto the prom and the sea breeze caught her dress and flirted with the hem. She pressed it down with her hand, and for the first time he noticed she was wearing her wedding and engagement rings.

He slid his fingers through hers, lifted her hand and pressed his lips to the rings, then freed his hand and offered her his arm. 'Just so you don't fall over and snap the heel off those shoes before I get to take them off you,' he murmured, and smiled as colour seeped into her cheeks.

'Nick!' she said under her breath, but there was a thread of laughter in her voice and she tucked her hand into his arm, the diamonds sparkling in the evening sun, and he laid his other hand over hers and walked her to the door.

To their astonishment it was opened by Leo, with the baby propped up against his shoulder held securely by his father's hand.

'What are you doing here?' Liv asked, sounding astonished.

'Amy wanted to show him off, so her mother's babysitting the girls for a bit, and we heard you were coming down so it seemed like perfect timing. We've only popped down for a few minutes. Come and join us for a drink, if you're not in a hurry to eat? We've just opened some excellent Prosecco.'

'No, we're not in a hurry but we don't want to intrude—'

'Don't be ridiculous. Come on, Amy wants to see you.'

Leo handed round the glasses, and they all toasted the baby who seemed perfectly content snuggled down in his father's arms. Leo looked pretty happy, too, and so did Amy, but it wasn't long before the party broke up because little Rocco was beginning to stir and Amy wanted to take him home and feed and change him.

'You know what it's like when they're tiny and your milk's just come in and everything hurts— I just don't want to do that in public yet!' she murmured.

'I can understand that,' Liv said with a smile, and kissed Amy goodbye, trying desperately hard not to be jealous. 'Don't forget, any problems, any questions, either ask your community midwife or give me a ring—I don't mind, any time. Here—my number.' She jotted it on an old envelope in her bag and handed it over. 'Now go and enjoy him.'

'We will. And thanks again.'

'Yes, thank you, both of you,' Leo added. 'I hope you enjoy your meal.'

The maître d' appeared at their sides with a welcoming smile and showed them to their table, and after they were settled Liv looked up and met Nick's eyes.

'I can't believe we're here.'

'No, nor can I. We tried before once—do you remember? It was impossible.'

'I don't remember that. I thought this was our first date?'

His brows tweaked together, followed by a slow, lazy smile as he propped his elbows on the table and leant towards her. 'So it is.' He reached out and took her hand, his thumb stroking softly over the back of it. 'Did I tell you how beautiful you look tonight?'

She felt herself colour. 'You may have done, but I don't mind hearing it again. You don't look so shabby yourself, either, and I see you've shaved.'

'Well, you see, my mother told me that it was

bad form for a chap to give a girl a rash on her lip from too much kissing—'

'Did she really?'

His sexy chuckle rippled over her and made her body quiver. 'No, of course not, but we should probably test the theory.'

'Sounds good.'

'I thought it sounded like a thoroughly *bad* idea,' he said softly, and she felt her pulse pick up a notch.

'Excuse me, are you ready to order or would you like a few more minutes?'

'Um—I think that would be a good idea,' Nick said, straightening up, and she had to bite her lip. 'Stop it and read the menu before we get chucked out,' he muttered, trying not to laugh, and she looked down and felt her eyes widen.

'Oh, my life, everything sounds amazing!'

'Doesn't it just? How many courses do you want?'

'Oh, two, max. I can't eat any more than that.'

'Main and dessert? I know you women like a pud.'

'Sounds lovely, and I wouldn't like to appear

greedy on our first date,' she said, her lips twitching, but he didn't smile back.

'You can have anything you want tonight,' he said, 'anything at all,' but his eyes said far more than those apparently simple words, and it took her breath away.

'That was the most amazing meal of my life.'

'Mine, too. I can't believe they wouldn't let us pay. Do you fancy a stroll?'

Liv looked down ruefully. 'I do, I'd love to, but they're not really strolling shoes.'

'No, they're not, are they? Maybe on our next date.'

She tilted her head and smiled. 'You want to see more of me?' she asked mischievously, and his mouth twitched.

'Definitely. A lot more.'

'Mmm. I want to see more of you, too.'

The light from the streetlamps caught the beating pulse in the base of his throat, and his voice was low and promising. 'I'm sure that can be arranged. Shall we go?'

She tucked her hand into the crook of his elbow, and he led her to the car, opened the door for her and went round to his side, starting the car in a silence screaming with tension.

Two minutes later they'd pulled up outside the cabin.

'There are no lights on in the house.'

'They're away,' he said, and she thought of the significance of that—the utter solitude, the privacy, no one to see or care what they did so they could be free to be themselves—and a shiver of need ran over her.

The cabin was softly illuminated by a bedside light, drawing her eyes to the bed. The curtains were closed, the bedding crisp and smooth, but not for long. Her pulse picked up and she turned towards him wordlessly.

His hands settled gently on her shoulders and he stared down into her eyes, his own intent and focused solely on her.

'I want you, Liv,' he said, his voice quiet but sure. 'I've never wanted anyone as much as I want you now, but if you're not ready for this, if you don't want it, then tell me.'

She met those serious, steady eyes, his gaze unwavering, and knew she'd never wanted him or needed him more. 'I want it. I want you, Nick.

I always have, right from the first moment I saw you, and I don't think I can wait any longer. Make love to me—please?'

His eyes closed briefly, and when he opened them again, passion burned bright in their depths. 'My pleasure,' he said, his voice little more than a breath that whispered over her skin, and taking her hand, he led her over to the bed and slowly, inch by inch, he drew the dress up over her legs, her body, her upstretched arms.

It fell to the floor in a shimmering puddle, and he stood back and looked at her, those hot eyes raking over her body and leaving a trail of invisible fire in their wake.

A fingertip followed, tracing the top edge of her bra, following a strap down from her shoulder, over the swell of her breast, dipping down into the hollow of her cleavage. It swept under the lace, trailing back up, his hand sliding in and following it until her breast was swallowed by his warm, clever hand.

His thumb flicked her nipple oh, so gently, and she gasped. So he did it again. And again, and all the time his eyes were locked with hers.

'Nick,' she breathed, her voice choppy, not

knowing what she was asking, but he knew, and he bent his head, his eyes finally releasing hers as his hand pushed the lace out of the way and his mouth found her breast.

His tongue flicked over her nipple, then circled it before drawing it into his mouth, and her hands gripped his shoulders, her breath sobbing now, the ache in her body so intense she could barely stand.

'Nick...'

He lifted his head, tugged back the covers and pushed her gently back until her legs met the bed. She sat down abruptly and he tipped her back, ran his fingertips around the top of her new and barely there lace shorts and peeled them slowly, inch by inch, down her legs.

He reached her feet, eased them over the shoes and then picked up one foot and ran his tongue over the inside of her ankle, up over her calf, behind her knee, then up, along her inner thigh.

She knew what he was going to do, knew just how good he was, how exquisite it would be, and she felt her body liquefy for him.

At the first touch of his tongue she dug her fingers into the bedding, biting her lips to stifle the scream, but she couldn't silence it and she could hear as well as feel his breath as it sawed in and out of his chest.

'Don't hold it in, Liv,' he said, his voice rough with need. 'There's no one to hear you except me, and I want to know exactly what I'm doing to you.'

'Nick, please...'

She felt the tug as he suckled, the flick of his tongue with its unerring accuracy, and she sobbed his name helplessly as her body peaked and everything shattered all around her like shards of light.

Then he was there, holding her in his arms, raining kisses on her face, his chest heaving against her.

'I need you,' he growled softly.

Her hands ran over him, finding silk and cotton where there should have been skin, and she plucked at his shirt. 'You've got too much on,' she wailed.

'So undress me,' he said, pulling her to her feet, but the buttons were too much for her so he hauled the shirt over his head himself. It landed on the floor near her dress, followed by her bra, their shoes, his trousers and socks and last, his jersey boxers. Her hand closed over his straining erection and a groan shuddered against her hair.

'Liv, no,' he begged, and she moved her hands to his shoulders, stepping back and meeting those fierce, white-hot eyes.

'I need you,' she said, her fingers curling into his shoulders. 'Please, Nick, I need you inside me—'

And at last—at last—he was there, thrusting deeply into her, taking her so close and yet not quite…

'Easy, Liv, easy. I won't last—'

'I don't want you to last. I want you to come with me this time, please, please…'

He drove into her then, every move of his body designed to wind her higher until she felt the starburst start again, spreading out and blinding her to everything but Nick.

He caught her scream in his mouth, his body stiffening as a ragged groan tore through him, and then as the contractions in her body died away he dropped his head against her shoulder, his cheek resting against hers as their breathing slowed and their heart rates came slowly back to normal.

Then he rolled to the side, taking her with him, their bodies still joined, and she opened her eyes and he was just there.

His lashes had clumped together, and she lifted a hand and brushed a tear from his cheek.

'Are you OK?' she asked softly, and he smiled, but it was a pretty sketchy smile and he couldn't stop the tears that leaked from his eyes and dribbled down onto her shoulder.

'I've missed you so, so much,' he said raggedly, and then she lost sight of him because her own tears flooded her vision, but she knew just where he was, and so she kissed him, and held him, and told him over and over that she loved him, until at last he fell asleep in her arms.

He woke in the night and made love to her again, but this time it was slow and lazy and tender, and they didn't wake again until the light filtering through a gap in the curtains cut a bright swathe across their pillows and dragged them out of sleep.

He propped himself up on one elbow and stared down into her eyes.

'Good morning.'

She smiled, a slow, contented smile that lit her eyes from within, and reached up a hand to touch his face. 'I couldn't agree more. It's a very good morning.'

'Mmm. I'm hoping it's going to get even better.' He lowered his head and kissed her gently, then swung his legs over the side of the bed and stood up, stretching hugely.

'Tea?' he asked, and she nodded.

'Lovely. Shall I just lie here while you wait on me?'

'You can. I was going to put the kettle on and then shower.'

'How big's your shower cubicle?' she asked, and he laughed and headed towards the bathroom.

'Not big enough for what you've got in mind.'

'You don't know what I've got in mind.'

'I'm sure I can have a fair stab at it. Just stay there a minute. I won't be long.'

He had the fastest shower on record, shaved—because he intended to kiss her a lot, lot more—

then cleaned his teeth and left the bathroom to find her standing by the kettle humming softly to herself.

He walked up behind her, slid his arms around her and cupped her breasts with his hands.

'You're all damp,' she said.

'Because I was in a hurry. The bathroom's all yours. Don't be long.'

Long?

She didn't wash her hair, because she wasn't convinced the cabin had a hair dryer and anyway, she had much, much better things to do with the time, but she showered, borrowed his toothbrush and cleaned her teeth and went back out to find him propped up in the bed with two steaming mugs on the bedside table.

'What kept you?' he asked with a lazy smile, and she crawled across the bed to him and kissed the smile off his face.

'So what now?'

It was much, much later. The tea had grown stone cold, and they'd showered again and put their clothes on, but although she might get away with the dress if they were to go out, the shoes were a bit of a giveaway.

'Well, if we're going to do anything other than lie in bed all day I probably need to go home and get a change of clothes. Shoes anyway.'

'We could go for a walk along the river wall.'

'We could. We used to love doing that.'

'We did. Right, let's go then, and see if you can get inside before Bert clocks you and asks what you were doing last night.'

She laughed at that. It was so unlikely she didn't even waste time worrying about it, but when they got to the house there was an ambulance outside Bert and Gwen's.

'What the hell's going on?' Nick said, and got out of the car. 'Liv, go and change and come back out. I'm going to see if they need help.'

He ran round the end of the hedge and in through their front door, and she let herself in, tugged on yesterday's jeans and jumper with a pair of flat pumps and went straight round to Bert and Gwen's.

She could hear them upstairs, and she ran up, calling Nick's name.

'In the front bedroom,' Nick called, and she

went in and found Bert on the floor with a paramedic holding his head steady while Nick massaged his carotid sinus.

'He's in SVT,' he said over his shoulder. 'Can you look after Gwen and follow us to the hospital? I'm going in the ambulance with them but I'm just trying to get this to work first.' She went over to Gwen who was standing to one side, her hands pressed to her mouth, and gave her a hug.

'It's OK, Gwen. He's in good hands.'

'Is he going to die?' she asked, and Liv could feel her trembling violently.

'I don't think so. Let's see if Nick can get this to work.'

'What's wrong with him?'

'His heart's started beating very fast. What Nick's doing is stimulating the nerve beside his carotid artery, which sometimes gets the rhythm back to normal. It's not hurting him, and it often works.'

Just then Bert groaned, and Nick stopped and laid his fingers over the artery and nodded.

'That's got it. Hi, Bert, it's Nick,' he said calmly, taking the old man's hand. 'How are you feeling?'

'Tired. Chest feels really tight. Need my spray.'

'He's got angina,' Gwen said, and she handed a GTN spray to Nick and then started to cry. 'I thought he was dead,' she whispered brokenly, turning her face into Liv's shoulder for a moment until she'd recovered her composure.

Liv found a box of tissues on the bedside table and handed one to her. 'Here. Mop yourself up and give him a hug,' she said softly. 'He's looking a better colour now. I expect they'll take him to hospital soon and sort him out.'

Gwen crumpled the tissue into a ball and crouched awkwardly down beside her husband, clutching his hand as Nick got to his feet and came over to Liv.

'Well done, you,' she said with a smile, and he pulled a face.

'Thanks. I thought it was worth a shot.'

'Definitely. Hadn't they tried?'

He shook his head. 'They'd only just got here. Once I said I was a doctor they just stood back and let me get on with it.'

'I'm so glad we came back.'

'Me, too. Are you all right to drive?'

'Yes, I'm fine. My head's perfectly all right

now, I just haven't bothered. I'll shut up the house with Gwen and follow you there.'

By the time they left the hospital it was almost one.

'Lunch?' Nick suggested, and she nodded.

'How about the pub on the river? We could go for a walk along the river wall afterwards.'

'Good idea. I'm starving.'

They went back to the house to swap cars and for her to change her pumps for trainers, and they ate lunch outside on the terrace overlooking the river, basking in the glorious spring sunshine and watching the boats swing lazily on their moorings.

'I could watch the river for ever.'

'Me, too. Shall we stroll?'

'Mmm. It might work off some of those gorgeous chips.'

'Don't work too many off. I rather like your new curves. It's like having the old you back again.'

'Well, ditto. You'd let yourself get flabby.'

'Flabby?' he said, sounding disgusted, and she laughed.

'Well, not flabby, that's going a bit far, but certainly not as toned and luscious as you are now.'

'Hmm. I like luscious better than flabby.'

'Me, too. I might have to check out your lusciousness again later.'

'Only if I can check out your curves.'

She gave him a cheeky grin. 'Be my guest. But maybe not here or now.'

CHAPTER ELEVEN

'So where are we spending the night?' he asked later when they were back at the house. 'Here, after we eat, or in the cabin?'

'I rather like the cabin,' she said, but then she frowned as they heard a car drive up, pause for a moment and then drive away after the door slammed, and she went to the window and saw Gwen letting herself in next door.

'Gwen's back. Should we offer her supper?'

Nick gave a wry smile. 'That would be nice—and if she's back, we really ought to be here. I don't like the thought of her on her own.'

Liv tipped her head on one side and stared at him. 'They drive you mad!'

He laughed ruefully and pulled her into his arms. 'I know, but they're harmless and he looked such a poor old boy, I just—they've been married for ever, Liv. What must it feel like to know you're getting near the end and one or other of you is going to go first? They'd be lost without each other.'

'I was lost without you,' she said, tipping her head back and meeting his eyes. 'So lost.'

'Me, too, but I'm back now, Liv, and I'm staying.'

'Good. And I know it won't necessarily be easy, but we can make this work, Nick.'

'Yeah. You're right. And if it gets tough, we'll just have to bite the bullet.'

'Wasn't that what people in the trenches used to do before their legs were amputated without anaesthetic?'

He laughed and drew her into his arms. 'I'm hoping it won't go that badly wrong,' he said, and then his mouth found hers and feathered a gentle kiss on her lips.

She looked up at him. 'So are you going to apply for the job?'

'Yes. Definitely. And I'll move back in here.'

'Sure?'

He kissed her again. 'Yes, I'm sure.'

'Even with Bert and Gwen watching our every move?'

'Even so.'

She felt the smile bloom in her heart and spread to her face. 'Good. Let's go and talk to Gwen and find out how he is.'

He moved back in the following day, while she was at work on a late shift, and when she got home that evening the light was on in his study.

It hadn't been on to welcome her home for so long, and her heart was filled with the sort of deep happiness and contentment that she'd only ever felt in their first years together.

There was only one thing missing, and she was used to that by now and it didn't dent her happiness.

He must have heard her car because he opened the front door, shut it behind her and pulled her into his arms.

'Welcome home, Mrs Jarvis,' he murmured, and it had never sounded so good.

He'd been working on his CV, he told her, and the next day he applied for the job, went through the formal interview process a fortnight later and found her in the ward office afterwards.

He pushed the door shut and let out a long, slow breath.

'God, that was tough. Ben really grilled me.'

'That was mean.'

'No, it was fair. They had a couple of very good candidates and the hospital seems to be able to attract them. This department's got a great reputation. I just hope I've done enough.'

She got up from the desk and hugged him. 'Of course you have. And if not, we'll go elsewhere. I don't care where I am so long as I'm with you.'

'What about our friends?'

She shrugged. 'We can make new friends. There's only one friend I'm really bothered about and that's you. Come on, let's go and get lunch, I'm starving. I've been waiting for you because we've got a lull, which means all hell's going to break loose later, so let's make the most of it.'

'There's a second interview round,' he told her the next day as he checked his phone over breakfast.

'Really?' Liv felt her stomach tighten, and she pushed away her cereal. 'Did you know that was on the cards?'

He shrugged and put his phone away. 'It was always a possibility. Oh, Liv, I hate this uncertainty.'

'It's only a job. There'll be others—and anyway, I'm still sure you'll get it,' she lied, her stomach in knots. 'I need to go, I'm due at work in a minute.'

'You haven't finished your breakfast.'

'No, I know. I'm not hungry yet, it's too early.' And she was way too stressed to worry about food. 'I'll see you later.'

The second interview was in three days, he told her later, and by the time it arrived they were both living on their nerves. The only thing that made it all go away was the time they spent together at night, when the lights were off and everything was quiet and she was in his arms.

Sometimes they talked, sometimes they made love, sometimes they just held each other, and in those times everything that was wrong seemed to right itself.

He got through the second interview, but that night he told her it was worse than the first and he was beginning to doubt Ben's friendship.

'Of course he's still a friend. He just has to be

your boss, too—he's the clinical lead and he's way too ethical to do anything other than give everyone the same treatment. You can be sure he was every bit as mean to them.'

'He wasn't mean, he just asked some really tricky questions—what would you do in this or that circumstance, that kind of thing. Really tricky cases where there's no definitive answer, and your brain just goes to mush.'

'I'm sure yours didn't,' she told him comfortingly, but the tension was getting to her and she wasn't sure she could stand the wait much longer. 'When will they let you know?'

'Ben said a couple of days, perhaps? I got the feeling the board were divided.'

She was off the next day, and because Nick was at work and she had to do something to keep herself sane, she went into her little study upstairs—the nursery that had never been needed—and settled herself down at the desk to read up on hypnosis as a form of pain relief in labour, but she couldn't concentrate.

Stress? Or an after-effect of her concussion? She didn't know, but it wasn't working, so she went downstairs, put the kettle on and reached for the instant coffee, then pulled a face.

She just didn't fancy coffee. Or tea, come to that. Or food. No, that wasn't true. There were some things she couldn't get enough of, like chocolate. And pasta. She could eat mountains of pasta and pesto. Maybe she was just hungry.

Or maybe she just needed to know what on earth was happening in their lives, and where their future lay?

She went for a walk, popped into the little local supermarket for some more bread and pasta and heading for the till she felt the blood drain from her head, and reached out and grabbed a nearby shelf. She'd walked down the aisle with personal products—feminine hygiene, condoms, pregnancy tests...

Pregnancy tests?

They were right there, in front of her. She'd bought countless numbers of them in that dreadful time, but she'd always done the test before her period was due, and if she'd only waited she would have had her answer for nothing.

But she'd lost track, between Nick coming

back and her accident and the job thing. She'd had one period, but that had been weeks ago.

More than four?

Her fingers shaking, she reached for a packet, put it in her basket next to the bread and pasta and went to the till.

'Liv?'

She must be out, he thought, and ran upstairs to change—and stopped dead.

Lying on the bed was the open packet of a pregnancy test.

His mouth dried and he felt sick. God, no. Not back to this again.

He changed into jeans and a thin T-shirt and sat down on the edge of the bed, staring at the open packet as if it was a bomb.

Why? They'd agreed on the rules—no trying, no thinking about it, no worrying, just accept that it wasn't going to happen for them without help and not until they were ready, but—no. She couldn't do that, and suddenly he wondered if she really loved him, really wanted him, or if it had just been a way of getting him back so she could use him as a stud, a sperm donor.

Jeez. He pressed his hand to his mouth, holding in the hurt, the rage, the overwhelming disappointment. The betrayal. And then he heard her call him.

He didn't want to answer. He'd promised they'd talk, promised they wouldn't let this destroy them again. Kick it into the long grass, she'd said, but there it was again, just when he'd burned his boats and taken the job, and he didn't know what to say to her because he didn't know if it was all a lie.

His heart in his mouth, he stood up and walked out of the bedroom.

'Where are you?' he asked, and followed the sound of her voice to the little room they'd never quite dared to call the nursery.

She was sitting at her desk, the test wand in her hand, and as he went in she turned her head and looked up at him and her face was streaked with tears.

'Why now?' he asked quietly. 'Just when everything was looking promising—why now, Liv? I thought we weren't going to do this?' he said, trying to keep a lid on his hurt, his anger. 'Dammit, you promised me we wouldn't do this!'

Her face froze, and she dropped the wand and stared at him. 'Nick—'

'No. I can't cope with it any more. I told you that, I warned you—'

He turned on his heel and walked out, and he was halfway down the stairs when something hit him on the head.

'What's *wrong* with you?' she sobbed. 'You can't cope with it when I'm not pregnant, and now, for God's sake, you can't cope with it when I *am*! What kind of a person *are* you?'

He slowed to a halt and turned and looked up at her. His heart was climbing out of his chest, his mouth was dry, and…

'I don't understand,' he said numbly. 'You can't be. I warned you my semen analysis was rubbish, we knew this wasn't going to happen—'

'No—no, Nick, you're wrong,' she said, shaking her head. 'Look at it! Look at the wand!'

He glanced down and saw it lying on the hall floor. His hand trembling, he bent and picked it up, and read the word in the little window.

Pregnant

He stared at it blindly, until the word blurred in front of his eyes. 'I don't understand.'

She came slowly down the stairs and sat just above him on the second step. 'I'm pregnant—we're having a baby, Nick. We're having a baby—'

Her voice cracked, and he looked up from the wand and met her eyes. 'How?'

She laughed then, the sound music to his ears. 'If you don't know that by now, Nick, you're *really* in the wrong job.'

He sat down next to her, his heart still pounding, and put his arm round her. 'But—why now and not then?'

She shrugged.

'Think about it. I was too thin, your diet was appalling, you were possibly drinking too much, having tons of coffee, not exercising, I was running every chance I had, we only made love when the techie runes told us to—and now we're healthy, we're relaxed, and we're making love every chance we have. It's not rocket science.'

She was pregnant. He felt the smile first, and then his eyes prickled and her face blurred, so he shut them and pulled her into his arms and held her, pressing his cheek against her hair.

'I thought you'd lied to me. I thought you didn't love me, you just wanted me back so you could keep on trying. I never dreamt...' He broke off to kiss her, then cupped her face in his hands and stared down into her eyes. 'I love you,' he said raggedly. 'I love you so, so much, and I can't believe it's finally happened for us.'

Her hand came up and stroked his cheek, wiping away the tears. 'Nor can I. Now if we could only hear about the job—'

'I have.'

Her mouth opened and she looked up at him, her eyes hopeful and fearful at the same time. 'And?'

'I got it. I got the job,' he told her, and she put her hand over her mouth and let out a sobbing laugh.

'Really? You got it? We can stay here in Yoxburgh, in this house, near all our friends, take our baby to the park...?'

'Yes. We can stay here. We sort of have to. I promised Ben we would.'

'Oh, Nick, that's amazing!' She flung her arms

around him and hugged him so hard his ribs crunched.

'Ouch.' He laughed, and eased her away. 'I'm glad you're pleased. We can celebrate that later. Right now I'm busy dealing with the fact that we're going to have a baby.'

Her eyes were soft, almost luminous, and her smile lit him up from the inside out.

'I know. I might have to share your study.'

'You might—if you have time for that when you're a mum. I still can't quite believe it's real.'

'I can't believe you've got the job, either. It's like we've reset the clock on our lives and gone back to where it all went wrong and put it right, and this is our reward.'

'Oh, Liv.' He hugged her again, then scrubbed his hands over his face and sniffed hard. 'I'm a mess.'

'You're a lovely mess. I was a very unlovely mess earlier, because I'd managed to convince myself that you hadn't got the job, and there we were pregnant and with nowhere to go and no visible means of support. It wasn't a good moment.'

'I'll bet. Poor you. How are you feeling now?'

'All right. I'm fine so long as I eat chocolate in industrial quantities,' she said, and he laughed again and hugged her.

'I'll add it to my regular internet shop,' he said drily, and then got to his feet and pulled her up. 'Come on, let's go and tell Bert and Gwen. Their grandchildren live hundreds of miles away, and I reckon they'll love having a baby next door.'

'Can you bear it?'

'What, them? They're fine, Liv.'

'Bert thinks you saved his life.'

'Well, he might be right. We'll let him think it. If he feels he came that close, he might let me take over the hedge cutting.'

She started to laugh, and once she'd started she couldn't stop, so he turned her into his arms and they leant on each other and laughed until their sides ached.

'Better now?' he asked eventually, and she nodded.

'Never better than this. The job, the baby, you back in my life for keeps—what more could a woman want?'

'Diamonds?'

'No. Cold, hard—and they don't hug you. I wouldn't swap your hugs for anything. Come on.'

She took his hand and stood up, only instead of heading out of the door towards Bert and Gwen, she turned towards the stairs.

'Where are we going?' he asked, and she just smiled.

'Up here. We've got a nursery to plan...'

EPILOGUE

NICK CLOSED THE door behind the midwife and went back into the family room, where Liv was curled up on the sofa in her towelling robe with the baby asleep in her arms.

'Cup of tea?' he asked, but she shook her head.

'I'm going to drown if I drink any more tea. Come and sit here and admire your daughter.'

She shifted her feet out of the way, then plonked them back on his lap as he sat down.

'Happy?' she asked him, and he gave a tired laugh.

'Yes, my darling, I'm very happy. A teeny bit stressed, but I might have known you'd want to be different.'

'I didn't plan a home birth. She was just in a hurry.'

'And I was in a clinic. I only got here by the skin of my teeth. I'm an obstetrician, for goodness sake, and I didn't even realise you were going into labour.'

'I'm a midwife. It's all I deal with, and I didn't recognise the signs. We're both rubbish.'

'No, we're not. We're amazing. Look at her. How could two rubbish people create anything as amazing as that?'

'Want a cuddle?'

He reached over and took the baby from her, staring down into her dainty, screwed up little face with its tiny button nose and rosebud lips. 'She's so perfect—such a miracle.' He looked up and met Liv's eyes and tried to smile, but it was too hard so he gave up.

'Have I told you lately how much I love you?'

'Only a million or so times.' She sat up with a little wince and put her arms around him and kissed him. 'But don't stop. I'll never get tired of hearing it.'

'I love you,' he said softly, and then propped his feet up on the coffee table, right over the tiny mark that he'd wiped clean, and rested his head back against the sofa and smiled at her.

Life had never felt so good…

* * * * *

LET'S TALK
Romance

For exclusive extracts, competitions
and special offers, find us online:

- facebook.com/millsandboon
- @millsandboonuk
- @millsandboon

Or get in touch on 0844 844 1351*

For all the latest titles coming soon,
visit millsandboon.co.uk/nextmonth

Want even more
ROMANCE?

Join our bookclub today!